CREAM OF KOHLRABI

STORIES

OTHER BOOKS BY FLOYD SKLOOT

LITERARY NONFICTION

The Night Side

In the Shadow of Memory

A World of Light

The Wink of the Zenith: The Shaping of a Writer's Life

NOVELS

Pilgrim's Harbor

Summer Blue

The Open Door

Patient 002

POETRY

Music Appreciation

The Fiddler's Trance

The Evening Light

Approximately Paradise

The End of Dreams

Selected Poems: 1970–2005

The Snow's Music

CREAM OF KOHLRABI

STORIES

FLOYD SKLOOT

TUPELO PRESS

North Adams, Massachusetts

Cream of Kohlrabi.
Copyright 2011 Floyd Skloot. All rights reserved.

Library of Congress Cataloging-in-Publication Data

Skloot, Floyd.
Cream of kohlrabi : stories / Floyd Skloot.—1st ed.
  p. cm.
ISBN 978-1-936797-10-3 (alk. paper)—ISBN 978-1-936797-05-9 (pbk. : alk. paper)
I. Title.
PS3569.K577C74 2011
813'.54—dc22

2011023779

Cover and text designed by Howard Klein.
Cover photographs by Beverly Hallberg. Used with permission.
Epigraph is from *The Collected Poems of Theodore Roethke* (Anchor, 1974).

First paperback and clothbound editions: September 2011.

Tupelo Press
P.O. Box 1767
243 Union Street, Eclipse Mill, Loft 305
North Adams, Massachusetts 01247
Telephone: (413) 664–9611 / Fax: (413) 664–9711
editor@tupelopress.org / www.tupelopress.org

Tupelo Press is an award-winning independent literary press that publishes fine
fiction, nonfiction, and poetry in books that are a joy to hold as well as read.
Tupelo Press is a registered 501(c)3 nonprofit organization, and we rely on public
support to carry out our mission of publishing extraordinary work that may
be outside the realm of large commercial publishers. Financial donations are
welcome and are tax deductible.

NATIONAL
ENDOWMENT
FOR THE ARTS

Supported in part by an award from the National Endowment for the Arts

For Beverly

I learned not to fear infinity,
The far field, the windy cliffs of forever,
The dying of time in the white light of tomorrow,
The wheel turning away from itself,
The sprawl of the wave,
The on-coming water.

—*Theodore Roethke, from "The Far Field"*

Contents

I

II

III

I

PLANS

They were coming to help him die, but Benjamin Dodge wasn't ready to die. He was thinking about a ten-day fishing trip to Alaska before the weather got too cold. Then it might be fun to attend his fiftieth class reunion back in Pennsylvania, see the campus again in autumn, all those elms turning red and gold. See what it was like now that women were enrolled. For mid-winter, France was a possibility. Lousy weather, sure, but there were good rates over there in February. Living most of his life in Oregon, Dodge was used to lousy weather. Best of all, he had three great seats behind home plate for the opening night game up in Seattle, Mariners against the Red Sox. He'd already bought the Seattle plane ticket and was going to arrange for one of those vans to take him out to the Portland airport April 2. As always, Dodge had plans.

His son Dustin would meet him at Sea-Tac before the game. Dusty and the little boy, what was his name? Eddie? Ethan? Etienne, that's right. Dodge knew he'd never get used to the moniker. Etienne Achille Tissot-Dodge. Poor kid. That's what you get when your dad marries a Parisian architect. How in hell did they

3

expect Dodge to remember a name like that? Had nothing to do with getting old or being sick. French was an impossible language. Dodge could use a little less rolling of the eyes from his son's wife, Jeanne-Marie, when he butchered the pronunciation. He was usually in the right neighborhood, at least, and had gotten some of the basic words down, the essential vocabulary. Though to tell the truth, he didn't mind when Jeanne-Marie rolled her eyes at him. She was a fine mother to Etienne, a fine wife for Dusty, and had those huge, luscious brown eyes. No: *Lustrous*, that was the word. Dodge was lucky, he knew that. A beautiful family. It would be good to see them again. Jeanne-Marie would have packed them a lunch, not understanding that eating ballpark food was part of the experience. Even at this new Safeco Field, where the food was lousy and so dangerous that the health department kept threatening to shut the vendors down. What the hell, as long as they were open, the food was safe. Buy his grandson a hot dog if he wants one, *oui?* Throw the lunch out. It would be great to be in an outdoor ballpark again, now that the Kingdome was closed. Make him feel alive!

Dodge understood his diagnosis. Terminal lung cancer. Nothing to be done, the doctor had made that quite clear. As had Justine, Dusty's twin, bless her candid heart. Now Justine had arranged for a leave from her state job down in Salem and was moving in with Dodge. Coming home, which he'd wanted Justine to do ever since her husband ran off three years ago. But not like this. Not to watch her father leave, too. Nothing to be done.

He couldn't remember if Justine was supposed to be here before the hospice people arrived. Probably she would. She'd been with him each step along the way so far. Dodge remembered her sitting beside him on the hospital bed as the doctor explained everything. She kept nodding and taking notes, clacking away on that little laptop she carried all the time, bent over it on her lap like the schoolgirl Dodge remembered. He found it difficult to listen to the doctor because of seeing Justine's hair hanging down in front of her face and shielding her little computer screen, seeing her legs folded together on the bed to make a nook for her work. Suddenly it was the winter of 1969 all over again and Justine was twelve, and Dodge found himself wondering where Dusty was.

Then Dodge was back in the room and back in 1999, listening to Dr. Stutzka. Name sounded like a Nazi war plane, which wasn't a good sign. Yes, things were quite clear. Dodge was going to die. He knew the cancer was in his lungs and had gone up to his brain. Why else would he forget his own birthday? Why else would a steak suddenly taste like compost, or would he stumble when the wind direction changed, or get lost backing out of his own garage? He knew *something* was wrong with his brain, but at first he'd thought Alzheimer's. Scared the hell out of him. Which was probably good, because then cancer sounded a lot better. The way the doctor said that, about it spreading to the brain, Dodge knew it was probably grabbing everything else in its way too: heart, esophagus, throat, maybe even his damn teeth, which hurt all the time now. The cancer had him like that giant squid in the Jules Verne story he used to read to the twins. No, wait, cancer was a crab. Oh well. The twins were so terrified of that story and yet kept asking him to read it. At night, no less, right before going to sleep. He could just see their faces the time he took them to Alexis's Restaurant downtown and ordered calamari for an appetizer. Oh God, Dodge did love raising the two of them.

Advanced metastatic cancer. Secret killer. Dodge had waited too long. But how was he supposed to have known what was going on? He had allergies and he'd always coughed, wheezed. He'd been tired for eight years, so what was a little more fatigue? And he'd stopped smoking. Several times, in fact, so he never suspected lung cancer. It just seemed to Dodge like he was getting old young, but some people do. Hair turns white overnight, skin folds up around itself, age spots and warts start popping out, and there you go.

Doctors don't like to give patients a timetable anymore. None of this *You've got six months to live* business. They prefer to say that the body's unpredictable, even with cancer this widespread. Nevertheless—that was the very word Stutzka used—Dodge was wise to forgo further treatment. Pointless suffering. Stutzka said he could make Dodge comfortable and, after all, who really knew how long it would all last? It was best to enroll in the hospice program, let the nurses and the social worker ease his way, and that's where Dodge stopped listening and happily went back to 1969.

He knew it was 1969 because that was the year Justine wore the same lavender hair-ribbon every single day and spent every single evening working on her poetry. Scratching away in a journal on her lap. Dusty wore a matching ribbon in his equally long hair, and, while he didn't write poems, he worked every single evening on his Manifesto. Lavender in his hair, Radical Manifesto in his lap, and a big fat grin on his lovely, smooth face. Dodge would sit downstairs with his wife Augusta trying to read travel books while she knitted and they both endured the same songs over and over from upstairs. "Crimson and Clover." How Dodge hated that one. There was a group called Brooklyn Bridge that had a hit then too, but the kids didn't like that one. Maybe *it's the best thing / for you / but it's the worst that could happen / to me.* He remembered looking up from his book to find Gus's foot tapping to the goofy beat while the rest of her seemed closed down around her needles. It was a strange time, all right, and the twins seemed to be preparing for flight, just counting the days till they were old enough and bold enough to fly up, up, and away.

Except it turned out to be Gus who flew away. First to a commune in upstate New York, then to the left-hand corner of New Mexico, and finally to a deserted beach west of Guadalajara where her clothes and empty purse were found. Suicide? Murder? The case was closed almost before it had been opened. Dodge hadn't known there was an official process for declaring someone dead even if there was no body found and there was no evidence of death or foul play. A long process, true, but official nonetheless.

Dodge had finished raising the twins himself and, when he began to travel, had to convince people that he wasn't trying to track Gus down. But he knew she was dead. Didn't need further evidence because he'd dreamed it the night she disappeared in Mexico, before he ever heard she was missing. Finally, about two years ago, a woman who had been traveling with Gus wrote to say that it was true, Augusta Harrington Dodge had died on the beach after accidentally ingesting poison mushrooms that she thought were mere hallucinogens. Stripped, ran into the surf and was gone. The woman was sorry she'd waited so long to write, but she'd only just now gotten over her grief.

At that point in his rambling memories, Justine had taken his hand and dragged him back to the present, to the bed in the hospital where Stutzka droned on. She had tears in her eyes, but a smile on her face as if suspecting he'd just been visiting them back thirty years earlier.

"You understand all that, Papa?"

"Not a word." He'd pointed to her computer. "But I can read about it at my leisure."

Justine had driven him home from the hospital and made all the necessary calls. She got him set up with the right kind of bed, bought a new television whose picture he could actually see across the room, filled the prescriptions, agreed with somebody over the phone about equipment they'd need, and said she'd be back in time to meet the hospice team. That's right. She was coming home before the ghouls arrived.

All right, Dodge knew he was going to die. Sure, he might even be dying right now, in a manner of speaking, or at least more so than most people are, from minute to minute. But he wasn't through living yet, and had only gotten home from the hospital two days ago, so what was the rush here? He had plans, damn it. Letting these hospice people into his living room seemed like ushering in the Reaper himself. But Dodge was too polite to turn them away.

What did they mean, it was March already? It was too warm for March. What happened to the fishing trip and the alumni weekend? What happened to France?

Except for his cold feet and hands, which seemed stuck back in the winter he'd apparently missed, Dodge felt too warm. He was sure it was July. August, at the most. But from his new bed he couldn't see out the window for verification. What had they done with his window, anyway? He looked around and realized he was downstairs, not upstairs, and in a bed in the den, for God's sake.

"Light," he said, and then fell asleep for a while.

He woke up thinking about July. Must have been 1970, give or take. The time Justine and Dusty went to horseback-riding camp in the Siskiyous. Dodge had driven them down there, six hours in the summer heat, and almost passed out when he saw how primitive the camp conditions were. All he needed to hear was one complaint from either of them and he would have taken them back home. But they seemed thrilled. Couldn't wait for Dodge to leave so the fun would start. Within a week they'd called begging to come home. Bad food, crabby horses, nasty counselors, relentless heat, kids fainting out of their saddles. That time, it only took Dodge five hours to get there. July. How could it be March now?

And who were these women scattered around the bed? Where was Justine? And what hurt so bad?

"Mr. Dodge?"

"Ben."

"Mr. Dodge?"

"I said call me Ben." He sat up. "Who are you?" Whoever she was, she was pretty enough to sit there at the foot of his bed as long as she wanted.

"We met on Friday, don't you remember?"

"Oh, yeah, I remember you." Who the hell was this? "Sure."

"Carrie Lillis, the social worker from Hospice." She smiled and Dodge wondered if someone had opened a window after all. He thought, *Do that again, my dear.* She reached for his hand and said, "We talked, and you signed some forms. But you were too

9

tired so I came back today like I said I would. I wanted to see how you're doing."

"Tell you the truth, Lily, I don't know how I'm doing." He coughed and reached for his handkerchief, which wasn't in his pocket. In fact, his pocket wasn't even on his shirt, which confused him. "Where's Justine?"

"I'm out here, Papa." Now he could hear her clacking on the laptop. She must be in the dining room, if this is the den.

"Mr. Dodge, you seem to be in pain. What hurts?"

"Ben."

"When? Well, right now. Where's your pain?"

"I'd have no pain if you smiled again."

Carrie Lillis patted his hand. Dodge thought she had truly amazing eyes, the sort of blue he'd seen within the dark mask of an Alaskan husky. Astonishing, otherworldly eyes. When she smiled, they widened rather than narrowed. He felt sure he could trust this Lily.

"Do you know what the date is?" she asked.

"Funny you should ask. I've been having some trouble with that."

Justine stuck her head into the room and said something Dodge didn't catch. Lily got off his bed, lodged her pen sideways in her mouth and disappeared. Dodge blinked. Then she stood up with some papers in her hand, so he figured she'd just bent down to fetch them from her briefcase. He didn't like it when people vanished. He wanted to keep his eye on everyone all the time. He watched her walk across the room to join Justine and as the women read Lily's papers together, Dodge thought about something he hadn't thought about in years: the smell of leather. He loved to lug around his fancy briefcase, clean and polished, as he visited prospects or clients, settling down to talk with them, unpacking his forms and documents. He loved the way his briefcase sounded like a saddle when opened. Buffalo Ben Dodge, Insurance Man. Nothing like the scent of good leather. Now everything smelled the same, like rancid chicken liver.

Lily was back. Had she really gone over to huddle with Justine? She asked, "Is there anything you need?"

What a strange question. *Well, I need not to have cancer. I need to breathe without this thing stuck up my nose. I need a good laugh and I need it to be, say, 1969 again despite the music. I need more time.* He closed his eyes.

℮∿

Justine was sitting on his bed again. She wasn't bent over her laptop, but Dodge still thought he could hear clacking.

"Are you cold, Papa?" She pulled his blanket up and tucked it around his torso.

"I'm hot."

"Well, you're shivering." She sprawled across his body as though to add a layer of warmth. No, now he understood, she was hugging him. "Your teeth are chattering."

It was ridiculous. Worse than that, it was humiliating. Not only were there parts of himself he no longer had control over, there were parts Dodge no longer seemed connected to at all. He hadn't even known he was shivering. And he was already wearing diapers, which poor Justine had to change. She was having to mother her own father. Not that she complained, but still, Dodge

11

hated what was happening. At least, he hated it when he understood what was happening, which wasn't often now, and then half the time he forgot what happened altogether. There was talk of a catheter soon, and no matter how hard he tried Dodge wasn't able to forget that.

He had no idea how many evenings they'd spent like this so far. Dodge would be propped up like royalty among countless pillows, dulled by pain medication and listening to Justine talk or read. Reading to him! Dodge was pretty sure she'd read him *The Call of the Wild* the other night. What next, *The Cat in the Hat?*

Everything was blurring together. Still, Dodge remembered and was sharply focused on that ball game coming up in Seattle. That's what made all this worthwhile. Just ten days away now. He had the tickets on his bedside table so he could see them. There'd been some talk about being realistic: No way he could ride into Portland in a van, haul himself aboard a plane, fly up to Sea-Tac, bustle through the airport, ride to Dusty's place, go to the ballpark. Nonsense. Dodge had done much more than that in his day. Okinawa, for instance. He knew what it was like to carry on when you were half-dead. To carry on for yourself and for your buddies, damn it. Hadn't he lugged Harris Olson across that godforsaken island on his shoulders? Don't tell Benjamin Dodge what he can and can't do. For the next ten days, he planned to rest hard. Industrial-strength resting. He planned to conserve his strength. Dusty was calling every couple of nights and Dodge was getting to talk with Etienne and Jeanne-Marie. It was all going very well. He felt much better knowing Dusty and Jeanne-Marie had a thriving practice now, more contracts than they knew what to do with, which was why it was so hard for them to come down and see him as often as they'd like. He wished they'd explained it all to him before. The boy was doing well in school and getting ready to play Little League baseball. He'd need a nickname though. Couldn't be Etienne on a ball field, no way. Too bad the kid's initials spelled "eat."

"Are you all right, Papa?"

"This medication makes me drowsy all the time. Diffused. Wait a minute, I mean confused. See?"

Justine didn't say anything, so Dodge wondered if he'd remembered to speak. "I want to back off a little, okay?"

"I'm not sure that's such a good idea."

She speaks! Dodge didn't have strength to waste in arguing, but he hated to be curt with her. He nodded, but could tell immediately that she'd misunderstood and thought he was agreeing with her. "No, I want to cut back. I'd rather be alert and in pain than asleep all the time."

This time it was Justine who nodded, so he thought he'd gotten through. But when she looked up at him, Dodge could tell she was on the verge of crying. "Are you afraid?" she asked.

"Pain doesn't scare me."

"That's not what I meant."

"Oh." Dodge struggled to collect his thoughts. He'd spent most of his adult life selling insurance. He was, himself, fully prepared for death from the standpoint of leaving something substantial for the twins. Affairs in order. His will updated, funeral and cremation paid for, neat step-by-step instructions prominently displayed on a legal pad inside his desk. Of course he wasn't afraid to face death. What did Justine mean by that? He'd made a living out of the business of dying, as though practicing for it, a career as morbid and necessary as an undertaker's. Well, now that it was gaining on him, in fact breathing down his own neck, Dodge didn't think he was frightened. There was still time. For what? That was the point exactly. "All I'm afraid of is not seeing what happens next."

Dodge knew he didn't want to miss that opening night Seattle ball game. He knew he wanted to see Justine settled on her own, or better yet: settled with a decent man in her life. Dodge knew that wasn't fashionable, he wasn't supposed to equate being married with being settled, but it was how he felt. He didn't want to miss his daughter's family happiness. But it looked like he'd have to die before she felt free enough to try living again.

The way days were spilling together now was like a foretaste of the hereafter. Dodge knew what he was afraid of: He was afraid the game would just slip away unnoticed and that would be a disaster. "Did Dusty call?"

In the middle of the night, the whole house hissed. At first, Dodge thought it might be Justine's breathing, but the sound was too steady. You have to inhale sometime, and this sound was all exhale. Like gas, or a faulty radiator, but he knew the house had neither. So what was it, did the River Styx steam? Was Dodge in serious trouble with the Lord?

Not only did the house hiss, it moved. Shifted weight and groaned like a man in pain, as though it had somehow taken on Dodge's burden for itself. There was something else, too. Something he knew he'd better not tell Justine or beautiful Lily when she came to check up on him. Elves. Fairies. Little People. He saw their faces wherever the heads of nails were supposed to be. All along the walls, up and down beams, as well as across the ceiling. They moved, sometimes. They chewed. Maybe they were hissing too, Dodge hadn't thought of that before. Probably these were the *sidhe* that his Irish friend Michael Farrell used to talk about in the bar after work. Pagan gods of the earth or some such nonsense. Very important to appease the wee fellows. Dodge would never have guessed they were real. So far, they hadn't bothered him, but he did like to keep his eye on them.

Time had really fallen apart on Dodge. Days roared by in great waves, but then sometimes there were nights like this where quite obviously time had stopped altogether. Maybe this is what it's like to be dead, Dodge thought. Frozen in time, unfortunately as a sick old man. How bad would that be, as opposed to simply vanishing, as he'd assumed he would? Poof! Like Gus: vanished to nothing except other people's memories.

Then, as though a hole had suddenly opened up in time, Dodge was at a ball park sitting between the twins in harsh sunlight. Where was this? When? Shading his eyes, Dodge looked onto the field and though his vision was hazy, as if his eyes had been smeared with Vaseline, he could see vivid spots of red moving around the field. Poppies in the wind. Right, he knew now: St. Louis, Missouri, and these were the Cardinals on the field with their bright red caps. St. Louis, so it was 1963 or 1964, the only time they'd lived in the Midwest. He was instantly happy, and he knew Dusty and Justine were happy too, and this was all he'd ever wanted.

"Justine?" he called. He hadn't meant to. She needed her sleep. He dozed and then his daughter was there, her weight causing the edge of his bed to sag slightly, as though they were together in a canoe. She leaned over him and adjusted his oxygen flow.

"Morning, Papa."

"Do you remember being out in a canoe with me on that lake in New Hampshire? You couldn't pronounce it for the life of you. Winnipesaukee. Every time I said the name, you'd laugh so hard I thought you were going to fall out of the canoe. I taught you how to paddle that day, how to do the J stroke and feather the water. How old were you, eight? Nine?"

"That never happened, Papa. I've never even been to New Hampshire."

"Well, who was in the canoe, then?"

"Must've been Mama."

Dodge shook his head, but he fell asleep before he could say, "Never!"

But sure enough, there was Gus in the canoe with him. Finally, she's come back, Dodge thought. Just what I need. Except he could see she was young, and her hair was its deepest red, like in the year or two after their marriage but before the twins were born. He could see himself from above, the fine hair light in the glare, but just as he tried to determine if the hair was blond or gray he found himself inside himself, looking out at Gus. What did that mean? Was this a memory or a vision? And wait just a minute here: Gus was paddling, not Dodge. That had to mean something. She'd come to take him away. He had to wake up! He had things left to do.

When Dodge opened his eyes, he thought he must be lying face up in a forest. All those heavy-leaved trees. No, wait, they had faces. He recognized Justine, right there. There was Lily, and beside

Lily was the hospice nurse whose name he never quite caught. And who's that? Dusty!

Dodge struggled to sit, but Justine gently held his shoulder down. "Let me crank the bed up instead."

He wished he could stay conscious. But after hearing Justine, the next thing he knew, Etienne was breathing next to Dodge's face, Jeanne-Marie was looming over the boy's thick black hair, and Dusty rose above her. Three bubbles in the air. It occurred to Dodge that this wasn't necessarily a good thing.

"Where am I?"

Then the television was on, the bed was filled with his family, Lily was gone and the nurse was hovering in the corner of the room. She was fussing with something Dodge couldn't see. He wondered: A picnic? Some kind of spread over there. Bottles, bowls.

"He's awake," Etienne said.

Dodge noticed that the boy had on a black and silver Seattle Mariners hat. It was too big for him and had settled low on his head, pushing out his ears. There was a light fuzz of dust around his lips, sugar maybe, or salt, something he was licking. What a lovely boy, Dodge thought. Who's he look like? A little of his French mother in the eyes and nose, perhaps, but taken together he's the image of his grandmother Augusta. Imagine that. She was here after all.

"Look over there, Pop," Dusty was saying. "We've got the game on for you."

He'd made it! Well, sort of. He sure hoped this wasn't some kind of joke. Maybe it was a videotape of an old game, or one of those meaningless exhibition games he never liked to bother with. Dusty wouldn't do such a thing. Not in front of the boy. Dodge knew he'd done a better job than that raising Dusty.

"Who's winning?"

Dodge tried to glance at the light, but he couldn't move. That was all right. It was just fine to lie here and gaze at Etienne. But Dusty didn't sound right. There seemed to be something in his throat. Now he was whispering. The two of them, the twins, always had their own special language, clicks and whispers that he and Gus could never decode. Still at it. And his eyes were red. Allergies, always had allergies, just like his sister. There she was, same thing, red eyes and the nose like a clown. Jesus, they're crying. Mariners must be losing. No, Dodge thought, I really must be dying.

"Don't worry, we win," Dodge believed. He drifted away before anyone could speak, but he knew he was right.

Alzheimer's Noir

It was about ten at night when I saw her walk out the door. Now they're telling me that's not what happened, she wasn't even there.

I don't buy it. The room was dark, the night was darker, but Dorothy was there. We were in bed and her curved back was against my chest. She wore the pale yellow nightgown I love, with its thin straps loose against the skin of her shoulders. My arm was around her, my hand cupped her breast, we were breathing to the same rhythm. Then she slipped from my grasp and I felt a chill where she'd left the sheets folded back. She drifted like a ghost over the floor, down the hall, and out the front door that's always supposed to be locked. I saw her fade into the foggy night.

They tell me I'm confused. What else is new? I'm also tired. I have a nasty cough from forty-six years of Chesterfields, even after two decades without them. And don't sleep worth a damn, which is why I saw what I saw in the night. Confused, maybe, but the fact is that Dorothy is gone.

e~

For three, four years now, Dorothy is the one who's been confused. That's what we're doing in this place, this "home." She has Alzheimer's. We had to move out of the place where we'd lived together for around sixty years.

"Jimmy," she'd say to me, "you look so much like Charles."

Well, I *am* Charles. Jimmy's our son, gone now forty-two years since he went missing over Cambodia, where he wasn't even supposed to be.

It broke my heart. Filled me with despair, all of it: Jimmy gone too soon, then Dorothy slowly leaving me, now Jimmy somehow back because of her confusion so I have to lose them both again, night after night.

$$e \curvearrowright$$

I miss her. Where's my Dorothy? I saw her walk out the door that's supposed to be locked. Because Alzheimer's people wander. They try to get out of the prison they're in, and who can blame them. I feel the same way, myself.

But at eighty-two I still have all my marbles. Thank God for that. Memory? Obama, Bush Junior, Clinton, Bush Senior, Reagan, Carter, then what's-his-name the football player, then Nixon, Jackson, no, Johnson. Kennedy, and I could go all the way back to Coolidge but I don't want to show off. Or I could do 100 93 86 79 72 65 and so on.

I saw her fade into the foggy night. The staff here can't remember to lock the front door, and I'm supposed to believe them when they say that what I saw with my own eyes didn't happen? It's a crime, what they did. What they're doing. Negligence. It's like they're accomplices to a kidnapping. Anything happens to Dorothy, I hold them accountable.

Truth is, I'm not sure how long she's been gone. I thought it was only a few hours, but then I look outside and see the day's getting away from me. Dark, light, dark again. Makes me weary.

"Let me use the phone," I say to Milly, the big one, works day-shift.

"Sorry, Mr. Wade. I'm not authorized to do that."

Always the same thing. "Look, Dorothy wandered away! No one here's doing it, so I need to call the police and file a missing persons report."

"What you need is a rest."

"What I need is a detective."

Milly shakes her head. "We've been through this ten times today."

The phone is in a locked closet. She tests the door on her way to the kitchen.

I saw Dorothy fade into the foggy night. They tell me that's not what happened, she wasn't there, but I don't buy it. Her curved back against my chest, the chill, her long white hair fading as she drifted like a ghost over the floor, down the hall, and out.

℮

Well, okay then, it's up to me. I'll have to find her myself. Be the detective myself.

Why not? I'm used to hunting around, discovering lost old things. Forgotten old things. For fifty-plus years, I had my own antiques business here in southeast Portland, just a short walk from

Oaks Bottom. Sellwood, the neighborhood's called, and that's just what I did: sold wood. Found my niche with bookcases— Italian walnut, mahogany, inlaid items with wavy glass doors— then other library furnishings, and rare books eventually. Always liked antiques. I just never planned on turning into one.

Wait a little while longer till it gets dark, till the other residents are in bed and the night staff is "resting" like they do. No doubt with a rum, a beer, whatever they drink. What I'll do is sit here in the old rocker, a perfect reading chair I found at an estate sale in Estacada, must have been 1948. Dorothy wouldn't hear of me trying to sell this thing. Nursed Jimmy in it.

I find her at the Dance Pavilion. I knew she'd be there. With her long lean body and long blond hair, she's easy to spot. Lights reflect off the polished wood floor that's marred by years of dancing feet. The low ceiling makes for good acoustics, and in the temporary silence I hear Dorothy laugh. I walk right over to her and take her hand.

No, that was 1945, just after the war. I'd met her two weeks before, and she told me where I could find her if I wanted to. Oaks Park, the Dance Pavilion, not far from the railroad tracks and the totem pole. I'm nineteen and it feels like it's happening right now. Like I'm at the Dance Pavilion with her hand in mine.

I wake up in the rocker, still eighty-two. Stiff in every joint, I creak louder than the old oak itself. What I need is a shot of good scotch. The kind that's been aged twelve years, the last two years in port barrels, say, with a hint of chocolate and mint. Nothing peppery. Even when she was going away into Alzheimer's, Dorothy remembered her stuff about scotch. I loved to kid her about it. The old dame knew her booze. How I'd love to toast her at this moment, to look across the room and see her gorgeous back exposed by one of those bold dresses she wore in the heyday, see her head turn so those green eyes twinkle at me, her hand rising to return my gesture, the amber liquid in her glass filled with light.

e⌒

I find her tucked against the bluff in Oaks Bottom, looking up at wildly whirling lights. Discs, that's what they are, silvery and thin as nickels, and they're maybe forty, fifty feet above the ground, spinning in circles, blazing with cold fire. Mesmerized, Dorothy doesn't see me yet. She can't take her eyes off them, these flying saucers. But I dare not risk calling out and alerting the figures moving toward her in the mist. Any luck, I'll get to her before they do. Before they can kidnap her and whisk her onto their ship.

No, that was 1947, when she was pregnant with Jimmy. Dozens of people down there in Oaks Bottom screaming, pointing toward the heavens, saying aliens were landing. All over Portland they saw these flying saucers. Cops, World War II vets, pilots, everybody saw them.

e⌒

I find her sitting with a half-dozen women on the bluff overlooking Oaks Bottom. All their chaise longues face north, upriver, with a clear view of Mount St. Helens. It's twilight, but steam plumes are clearly visible and what feels like soft rain is really ash. St. Helens has been fixing to erupt for months now.

Dorothy waves me over. She spreads her legs and flexes her knees, smoothing her flowered dress down between them, making room for me to join her on the chaise. I sit there on the cotton material she's offered to me and it's still warm from her body. I lean back against her, waiting for the mountain to blow.

No, that was 1980, when she was thinking the world might come to an end. Hoping it would, I believe. We were tired of it then, so you can imagine how we feel now.

No, we're not watching the mountain. We're watching Fourth of July fireworks from Oaks Park like we do every year. Surrounded by kids, happy kids, full of life.

Ah, Jesus.

e⌒

It's time to go find her. At least there's no rain. Always rains around here, often deep into June, and that would make it harder to track her. Not that a little rain would stop me. I have a warm jacket, a Seattle Mariners baseball cap, a flashlight. Nothing will stop me because I think this is it, the last chance. Because I don't know how long Dorothy's been gone. Floating down the hall. The dark. The night.

The only thing that makes sense is that she's lost somewhere in the woods again over in Oaks Bottom. That's her place, all right. One of the big reasons I decided to move into this "home" instead of some of the others we looked at was because it was in Sellwood and close to the bluff above Oaks Bottom. Clear days and nights, we can see across the wetlands and the little lake to the Ferris wheel and the roller coaster and the Dance Pavilion there at Oaks Park. Jimmy called it the musement center. Loved to ride the merry-go-round, spend a whole afternoon at the roller-skating rink. Sometimes now we hear the kids screaming as they spin or plunge on the rides. We hear the thunder of wheels on tracks. Lights flicker. I think Dorothy thinks it's him calling. Jimmy.

Even after Jimmy was gone, she liked to walk in Oaks Bottom. Not go over to the musement center, of course, but wander along the trails now that the city has turned all that land into a refuge. She'd stroll along the trail and name the trees: maple, cedar, fir, wild cherry, black cottonwood. I think maybe she was pretending to teach young Jimmy. Breaks my heart. She'd stroll along and smell the swampy odor, stumps sticking out of the shallow water, ducks with their ducklings. She'd. She. Then she.

Then she started to get lost in there. One time I found her walking past the huge sandy-hued wall of the mausoleum and crematorium, up at the edge of the bluff. How she managed to climb there from the trail I never understood. She was silhouetted against the eight-story-high building, its wings spread like a giant vulture. Or like the great blue heron painted against a field of blue on the building's center wall. She was drifting vaguely north, and I hated to see her there, of all places. I had nightmares about that for months afterwards. Another time I found her ankle-deep in water at the lake's edge, swirling her left hand through algae then looking at it as though she hoped her fingers had turned green. There were three little black snakes slithering around and over her right hand where it braced her body on the bank. One time I found her on the railroad tracks at the western end of the wetland. Just standing there like she was waiting for the 4:15 to Seattle.

Dorothy has stamina. I can't be sure where she might have gotten to this time. Or who might have found her and done something awful to her. Those neighborhood kids in their souped-up cars she always used to annoy, telling them she'd call the cops if they didn't slow down.

℮

I'm quiet leaving my room, quiet going down the hall, with its threadbare carpet, its dim lighting, quiet opening and closing the unlocked front door. But I don't have to be. No one's watching. I head off down the street like I'm going to buy a carton of milk, don't turn to look at any cars hissing by, just make my slow way toward the river and Oaks Bottom. It's not far.

On television, detectives always begin their investigations by going door-to-door asking the neighbors if they've seen anything. But I can't risk that. Start ringing doorbells around here, people will just call the "home" and say another old loony is on the loose. Turn me in. I'd be finished before I got started. Maybe when I get closer to Oaks Bottom itself I can find someplace to ask questions.

But after a few blocks, I have to stop and rest. The weariness just keeps getting worse. I think my only energy for the last few years came from caring for Dorothy. It's what kept me going. Without that, I'd probably be in the crypt by now, dead of exhaustion, locked away in the big mausoleum there overlooking the musement park. Or I'd be technically still alive but sitting in a chair all day while time comes and goes, comes and goes.

Now it's a few minutes later, I think. Could be more than a

few. Truth is, I'm not sure exactly where I am. But that's because my eyes aren't any good in the dark, not because I'm lost. I'm right above Oaks Bottom, somewhere. It's just that the landmarks are hard to make out. But there's a tavern here. I don't remember seeing it before. But it's so old, I must have seen it without noticing. Or noticed without remembering. That's what getting old is, I tell you, nothing but solitary seconds adding up to nothing.

I don't know how long I've been standing here. Or why I'm at this new old building. Squat little windowless place looks like it's made out of tin, painted white and red, with a tall sign in the parking lot: Bottoms Up. Then I remember: I should drop in for a quick minute and find out if anyone's seen Dorothy. Could have happened. The old dame knew her booze. Maybe she dropped in to the Bottoms Up for a quick scotch on her last rambling.

I take a deep breath. Which at my age is something of a miracle right there. And figure I have maybe another couple of hours before I have to head back to the "home," before they might start to miss me. So this can't take long.

I walk in, planning to sidle up to the bar and question the keeper. But the music, if that's what it is, is loud, and what I see stops me dead: two stages, one dark one light, and on the stage lit in flashing colors a naked woman with long light hair swirling as she gyrates above the money-filled hands of two men who look like twin brothers.

Is that? It's Dorothy! I'd know those broad shoulders anywhere. How could, No, wait, I blink and see now it's not her. Of course it's not. I'm confused. What else is new? But for a moment there.

I would give anything to see her again. To touch her again. To stand here near her again.

27

"What can I get you, old timer?" the bartender asks. He's twelve. Well, probably mid-twenties, pointy blond hair and a hopeful scrub of moustache.

I forget where I am, forget why I'm here. Looking around, seeing the dancer again, I say, "My wife."

He smiles. "I don't think so."

Then I'm walking through the parking lot, using my flashlight so I can access the trailhead and make my way down the steep bluff. I'm too old for this, I know it. All the walking could kill me, even though I'm in pretty good shape. But I can feel through the soles of my feet that Dorothy has been here, and even if it kills me I'm still going to find her.

A series of switchbacks gets me to the bottom, but I'm so turned around I'm not sure which way to walk. Time comes and goes like the wind, and I see the moon blown free of clouds as though God himself had turned a light on for me. It shines across the lake. Looking up through a lacing of tree tops, I see the now-moonlit mausoleum. So that's where Dorothy must be.

I begin walking north. Maple, cedar, fir, wild cherry, black cottonwood. The water makes a lapping noise just to my left. It sounds spent. Stumps sticking out of the shallows create eerie shadows that seem to reach for my ankles.

Rising out of the water, just beyond a jagged limb, I see a figure stretch and begin to move toward me. From the way it strides, I know it's my son, it's Jimmy. He wears some kind of harness that weighs him down, but he still seems to glide on the lake's surface, so light, so graceful.

Jimmy was never trouble, even when he got in trouble. That time, when the cops came to our door, it was only because he'd gone to protect his best friend, Frank. Johnny Frank. Or maybe Frankie John. I don't remember. A wonderful boy, just like my Jimmy, but a scrapper, and that one time he was surrounded by thugs and Jimmy went in there and—

Oh, Dorothy was so good with our son, all that time they spent at the musement park, and Jimmy lost his fear of the things he'd been so afraid of. Came to love the rides, the scarier the better. Of course, that's why he went into the service, why he ended up in flight school, why he ended up in a plane over Cambodia, shot down where he wasn't even supposed to be. Dorothy told me once it was all her fault. I took her in my arms, told her the only thing that was her fault was how wonderful our son turned out to be. And now look, here he is, still wearing his parachute harness, coming home to us at last.

"Come on, Jimmy. Help me find your mother."

"Where is she this time?"

I point toward the mausoleum. He follows my finger and nods, and just then the clouds return, and the mausoleum fades into the night, its sandy face turning dark before my eyes.

Jimmy can see anyway. He leads me and I follow. The trail rises and dips, follows the contour of the bluff. For an old man, I think I'm doing well with the tricky footing. Then I realize Jimmy is carrying me.

No, he's stopped walking and now he's the one who's pointing. We're very close to the mausoleum. Up ahead, standing against the building where Jimmy's ashes are stored, where my ashes will be stored, where—I remember now—Dorothy's ashes are stored, I see my wife smiling. She is leaning back against the wall just under the legs of that giant painted heron.

The wind rises. The clouds unveil the moon again and the building lights up. But no one's there after all. No one and nothing but a blue wall on which a hundred-foot-tall heron is preparing to fly toward heaven.

CREAM OF KOHLRABI

Ike Rubin sat on a loveseat glaring at the dining room doors. Three minutes before noon. They were double doors and Ike hated double doors. What was wrong with a good, old-fashioned door door, plain and simple? Also without the silly hexagonal windows up there where no one could see through. A door with one of those—

And there Ike had to stop. He hated when that happened. A door with one of those—what? Hands. No, damn it, not hands. One of those Nopples. The thing you turned to open the door.

But these double doors opened both in and out. Ike hated that. Make up your mind, door. Plus, they're not safe. Last month, he'd seen Charlotte Stern flattened by the Activities Director rushing out of the dining room a moment before the doors would be officially opened for dinner.

Actually, that hadn't been so bad. Charlotte deserved it, all the time trying to be the first one inside even though everyone had assigned seats, even though they didn't start serving till everyone was seated. What's the rush, anyway, with the crap they served here? If it's chicken on the menu, you can bet it's drumsticks.

Never white meat, don't be ridiculous, $1.39 a pound or whatever. Okay, maybe Charlotte wanted a head start on the bread. Still, you wait till the time comes. If Ike remembered anything from the camps, he remembered that.

He looked away, at a shadow moving across his periphery. Waiting was something Ike Rubin was good at. You didn't get to be eighty-nine by rushing. Still, he knew it was important not to linger either, because the ones who linger are the ones who starve. All right, there was an art to this, and even though Ike appeared to be lolling on a loveseat, he was paying attention. Always pay attention. But as far as he could see, everyone was still outside the dining room and lunch was late again. It figures. He returned his gaze to the doors. A door was supposed to have a transom and a lintel and a keyhole and stiles and a handle. A handle! There you go, that's what he'd been trying to remember. Across the lobby came Mrs. Astroth. No known first name. Ike hated that kind of pretension. What, he was supposed to call her Mrs. Astroth when she was five years younger than he was and wore hats Ike hadn't seen since 1932? Headed right this way, like he was wearing a sign saying Park Here.

"Hello, Mr. Rubin."

"Hello Mrs." Which was as far as Ike was willing to go. What did the woman want with him? Had he forgotten to say *Hello, Mrs.* out loud? He wished she wouldn't stand there blocking his view of the doors.

"Do you know what?" she whispered. "Can you guess who's coming to sing with us this Friday night?" She smiled down at him. "Finally."

"Mott the Hoople?" he said, remembering a group his daugh-

ter used to listen to. He remembered the name because Mott the
Hoople drove him crazy for two entire years. When was that?
1972 or so, he thought, because his daughter Rachel was still liv-
ing at home.

Mrs. Astroth tottered a little, as though struck by his words.
But didn't fall. She raised her hand to her modest chest in shock.
Ike blinked.

"What did you say?"

Ike tried to recall. Oh, right, she thinks I cursed, probably, and
wishes she could say *Mott the Hoople to you too.*

"I said What and who, Mrs. What and who are coming to
entertain us Friday."

Mrs. Astroth turned away, drifting toward a bank of chairs
against the wall by the windows, punishing him. So, he would
have to wait till Friday before finding the answer to this mystery.
This was all right by him. Then, over her shoulder, Mrs. Astroth
said, "Only Cantor Stanley Bloom, with his magnificent baritone
voice. That's who's coming on Friday evening. I've been asking for
them to book him since May of 1997."

Ike nodded. Of course, she was a little off her rocker. So who
here wasn't? He wanted to say *And all along I thought you meant
the Messiah was coming.* Better odds on that. Friday night, in lieu of
either Cantor Stanley Bloom, whose magnificent baritone voice
had been silenced since his death—in this very establishment—in
1974, or the Messiah, there would be another movie projected on
that tiny screen no one could see, with the sound so low no one
could hear it. *Now, Voyager,* for the seventy-ninth time, perhaps.
Didn't matter, Ike thought, most of them forgot the story by the
time the movie ended.

The Messiah. That's who Ike would request, if he felt like rising to the challenge. Bring on the Messiah, already, I'm almost ninety and I wouldn't mind being here to see Him. But Ike knew that management emptied the suggestion box every week and threw the paltry, futile scraps of paper away. He saw them do it. Cantor Stanley Bloom, my foot.

When the hell are the doors going to open!

He turned his head to check, and into Ike's line of sight drifted the beautiful Rosa Martinez. The woman is receptionist, pill dispenser, assistant manager, and postal deliverer all in one. Dressed, as usual, in white, so maybe she was a nurse too. Ike couldn't remember. She was always smiling, and today was no exception.

Ike struggled to rise. Such a person should be greeted with due respect. Also, people who walked right at you were sometimes armed, sometimes up to no good. If he remembered anything from—

"Hello, Mr. Rubin," Rosa said. "No need to get up."

Apparently she was right, because Ike's body stopped rising of its own accord and he sank back into the loveseat. He hated when that happened, but what could he do? He gathered his breath, thought about patting the vacant place next to him as an invitation for Rosa to sit, and tried to smile.

"Good morning, yourself. And you could please call me Ike, I've only asked you nine thousand times."

She held something out to him. "It doesn't say Ike on this. It says Mr. Isaac Samuel Rubin. That's you, if I'm not mistaken." She placed an envelope against his hand and he took it from her. "Ike."

He blinked at her and then looked down at the envelope. So who could possibly be writing to him here? It seemed as though

the only person in the world who knew Ike was still alive and re-
siding at *The Golden Sands* was his son Sheldon, who lived exactly
seven blocks away, which was too close to bother with mail but
apparently too far to visit his widowed father more than once a
month. There was a fancy, printed return address on the front of
the envelope, but Ike couldn't read it without his glasses and he
didn't want to put them on in front of Rosa, who had often com-
mented on how wonderful his vision seemed. If she only knew.
He could make out the general, hazy contours of things across the
room, which wasn't bad at eighty-nine, but he got by on a com-
bination of memory (fading), guile (holding steady), and patience
(decreasing). If there was one thing Ike had learned in the camps,
it was to know where he was at all times, without having to look.
Who needed eyes in places like those? He thought he would just
tuck the letter away in his jacket pocket and read it after lunch,
show Rosa how carefree and blasé an old man could be. It was
more important to talk to a beautiful woman than to read a letter
from someone he didn't think he knew.

But when Ike looked up, Rosa was gone. He checked his
jacket pocket to make sure there really was a letter in there. Maybe
he'd imagined the whole encounter. Letter in pocket. Scent of
Rosa's perfume still in air. Good signs.

Just then, accompanied by murmurs as in the first rustling
of a theater curtain, the dining room doors swooshed opened.
Ike rose, but waited till the first wave faded. When he'd come to
The Golden Sands Retirement Home a couple years ago, Ike had
made the mistake of entering the dining room in the vanguard
and was nearly swept off his feet, ending up beached at the far side
of the room, well away from his assigned table.

Now Ike settled at his table, across from Charlotte Stern. He put the paper napkin in his lap, snatched the sole slice of rye from the bread basket at the center of the table, adjusted his silverware. Soon the waiters were ladling soup from their tureens. Ike couldn't watch. Accuracy was a real problem for these guys. And none of the waiters spoke more than a few words of English, so maybe that's why they didn't respond to the abuse heaped on them at every meal. *Where's my tea? This soup is cold! The bread is stale the butter is too hard the chicken is rotten the ice cream tastes like sauerkraut the napkin is filthy you idiot.* After placing each bowl precisely before them, their waiter looked toward the windows, contorted his face into a miserable smile that pierced Ike's heart, and said, "Enjoy day's soup cream kohlrabi, please thank you."

As usual, he hadn't understood what the man said. But after the waiter moved on, Ike leaned over his bowl and was suddenly turned to stone. He couldn't budge. The vapors and the color and the texture taken together seemed to throw some kind of switch in his brain, rendering him lost in time and space. All Ike had wanted was the momentary pleasure of smelling the soup, and now he was filled with fear.

Without looking up, he asked, "What is this?"

"Cream of kohlrabi," Charlotte Stern said. "Not bad, for a change."

First of all, it had the odor of soil. Plus an unsavory cadaverish color, a chalky beige speckled with maggoty black. Could only be produced in soup, Ike thought, by a dangerous mixture of elements. He recognized in himself that familiar, deep uncertainty over what was in the food being served. Purée of Vomit chowder! With look, a sprig of expiring parsley at the edge of the bowl, where it seemed to be fleeing a yellow, toxic spill of fake butter. There was something foul, something alien here. In the camps, you never knew what they were letting you eat, only that it wasn't good for you. But after a while that didn't stop you from ravening down the poison. Hoarding trading stealing.

Where were these thoughts coming from? Ike thought he'd left them behind long ago. These seizures, or whatever they were. He had clamped down. He hadn't talked about his life in Europe to anyone since 1947, and he'd stopped dreaming about it, stopped having those night terrors. He'd buried it. Sheldon would ask and Ike would say *Sha! Don't worry about it.* Now look, everything reminded Ike again. Maybe it meant he was getting closer to death, though he felt fine enough. Instead of going ahead into the grave, it was as though he were drifting back to the grave, back to the camps.

So he did what he'd been trying to do every time, lately, when this sort of thing happened. He reasoned. Kohlrabi is what, a root? Like a turnip, only pale beige green. Or, he remembered, sometimes purple. Good thing they hadn't given him purple soup. All right, you take these strange little knobs which unfortunately resemble testicles, pare them down, throw them in boiling water. Then you do something with them, chop mash blend. Throw in some onion and garlic, maybe some chicken stock unless you're too cheap like the management here. A touch salt, a grind pepper, a plop butter. Ike also thought he might smell lemon. So that's all there is to it, right? What's to worry?

Cream of kohlrabi, Ike thought. Story of my life.

When the entrée arrived, Ike simply shook his head. Never fails. They serve perch that looks exactly like one of Sheldon's old sneakers from the closet, maybe two spoonfuls of peas and carrots heavy on the peas, and a corn on the cob. The people here, ninety-seven percent of them, have false teeth, and management serves corn on the cob. This, Ike thought, was a way they had of amusing themselves. If his eyes permitted, he was sure he would look up and find the staff gathered at the kitchen door watching as everyone tried to eat corn on the cob. Jack Levinsky had the right idea. Immediately took out his false teeth, wrapped them in a napkin, turned down his hearing aid and began gumming.

Ike was ready to leave, but he couldn't stand the thought of Muriel Rothberg, perched at the next table, claiming his uneaten ice cream. He'd seen her do that when Charlotte Stern left early to visit with her son, the eye-ear-nose-and-throat man. And the time Jack Levinsky got sick during lunch and couldn't eat his dessert, she'd snatched the dish off the waiter's tray before he could escape. So Ike sat there. Did Charlotte Stern's hair turn that shade of apricot because of the marmalade they served around here, which she couldn't stop eating? Plus, what did Jack Levinsky actually do when he went up to Charlotte's room after dinner? He would always shuffle over to the soda machine, buy one Diet Pepsi, then shuffle back to the elevator. He'd been seen by several people carrying the can into Charlotte's room like an offering, and she'd been heard by several people asking him *What took you so long?* But then the door closed, the sound of the television obscured whatever else might be said or done, and by 9:30 Jack was shuffling back to the elevator and down to his basement room.

This has to stop, Ike thought. It's like I'm gossiping with myself. He ate his ice cream so fast that it gave him a headache. Then he ran his hands over his shirt to flip the ends of his jacket back before standing, and felt the letter again. No way he was going to open it here at the table.

He walked across the lobby, considered sitting again in the same loveseat but thought it was too central, too open to scrutiny, and continued out toward the sunroom. Nobody sat in the sunroom after lunch because they all went to play cards in the Red Room. Ike liked being out here, and was annoyed with himself for failing to remember the sunroom more often. It fronted the boardwalk, the beach and the ocean, looking south toward, Ike thought, the end of the world. With the windows open, there was always the sound of the surf, a sound that Muriel Rothberg had been trying to get management to turn off for the last two years. Plus the smell of the sea, its briny air in the eyes and nose like the memory of crying.

He took out the envelope, struggled and failed to read the fancy embossed return address, then placed the paper face down on his lap. Checking to be sure he was alone, Ike fished out his reading glasses and put them on. Waldman, Widger & Weiss. Oh boy, Ike thought, the three Ws. The firm in which his brother-in-law Morris Weiss was a partner. Morris, his darling Molly's twin brother, he of the eyes nose mouth hands hair that were just like hers, the same sweet disposition. Morris Eliezer Weiss, Attorney-at-Law, whom Ike couldn't bear to see or speak to, even now four years after Molly's death. He'd refused to return Morris's calls, refused to give Morris his unlisted phone number here at the Golden Sands, refused to respond when Morris found it and called anyway. So now what does he want? This kind, gentle, how-could-he-be-a-big-time-New-York-lawyer that Ike missed terribly but had banished from his life. Sweet Morris would love the sunroom, Ike thought, just as Molly would have.

It was Morris that Ike had met first. Late June of 1947, start of the hottest summer that anyone remembered. Ike had been in America for a little over a year by then, and had found his way to a job on the docks and a bed in an East Flatbush apartment where his uncle lived. The first morning Ike awoke early in his uncle's place, Apartment 6B, and rode down on the elevator with Morris Weiss from 6E. Already, just past dawn, it was so hot that Morris was carrying the suit jacket over his arm.

They talked in the elevator and in the lobby and out on the street and Ike missed his bus. They met again that night after dinner and talked in the hallway between their apartments. By the end of the week Morris, the hotshot young lawyer, was helping Ike get employment in the supply room at the King's County Hospital, enrolling him in night school to study accounting, inviting him to 6E for dinner, schnapps. In early July, Morris was fascinated by reports of Unidentified Flying Objects being sighted all over the country.

"Look at this," he said to Ike, waving the newspaper before his friend's face. "A wingless disc was seen cavorting in the skies above California by an Air Force Captain and his wife. Then an alien craft crash-lands with a clap of desert thunder near Roswell, New Mexico. You have sightings in Wyoming, in Oregon, in North Carolina. All over the country, not just out west where you could excuse this kind of thing. What's happening, mass hysteria?"

"Aliens? You know that's what the British called us? Enemy aliens. We started showing up from the camps, some of us tried to get hold of our bank deposits, our inheritances from those who perished, and the British said we couldn't have them. We were still enemy aliens, after all we went through and with Hitler dead, the war over, the Allies everywhere you looked."

Morris put down the paper. He stared at Ike, looked away for a moment, coughed. "I didn't know that."

"Aliens."

Morris hadn't mentioned his twin sister until then. Molly worked as a nurse at the hospital. She was seeing a few of the camp survivors now as they came in for help with their damaged bones, their organs, their souls. He wondered if Ike wanted to meet some of them, talk to a few fellow survivors.

"For what?"

"It might help, Ike."

"If I never have to look at another face that has the camps written on it, I'll die a happy man." He forced himself to sit facing Morris and to smile. "But your twin sister, that would be another story altogether."

Now Ike turned the envelope back over. Without thinking, he resorted to his habitual letter-opening routine, withdrawing his key ring from its pocket, slipping the longest key under the envelope flap, and carefully tearing open the top. It was much better when you did things without thinking. Ike hated anticipation. But he couldn't help himself, and thought: I told him no mail. I don't hear from him for years, now this official correspondence. Ike knew this one was not the banned kind of letter, and that didn't make him feel any better. As he unfolded the stiff paper, he felt depressed, as though the document itself had released a wave of despair.

It was not from Morris at all, but from Adam Widger, the youngest of the partners. Ike noticed this right away, his eyes going to the signature first, and he knew in his heart that poor Morris had died. Of course, he was eighty-ish, Ike couldn't quite remember exactly anymore, but still. It was awful. Morris probably died thinking Ike was angry with him, or troubled in a way that their old friendship could not reach, or at least yearning for reconciliation. Nonsense, he told himself. You've almost watched too many movies you couldn't hear down in the Red Room. Besides, now that he read the letter, it said nothing about Morris being dead, just in Switzerland. Same thing, Ike thought.

There was, apparently, something called the Humanitarian Fund for the Victims of the Holocaust. Hundreds of millions. And there was now in place a procedure for eligible survivors to begin collecting money from this fund. Adam Widger was coordinating efforts for a group on the east coast, Morris Weiss was in Zurich advising a younger partner serving as liaison, and it was thought that Ike might be interested in having the firm assist him.

They send an octogenarian to Switzerland to talk to Nazi collaborators? They send a pussycat like Morris Weiss to deal with wolves and jackal-asses? Ike folded the letter, put it back in its envelope, put the envelope back in his jacket pocket, stood, sat down, closed his eyes, and fell almost instantly asleep. Rosa Martinez found him slumped over on the chair about twenty minutes later and screamed his name, thinking the worst, but her scream woke him and Ike sat back up, resting his head against the wall. He reached to touch the letter through his jacket, just to make sure it hadn't been a dream, and Rosa said, "What is it, Ike? Your heart?"

"I'm fine."

"Maybe it was your lunch, eh? Something didn't agree with you."

"Rosa, the cream of kohlrabi nearly killed me, but I'm dandy now. Just tired."

Rosa came over and actually sat next to him. Ike knew he

must look bad. The pretty ones never sit beside you unless you're on death's door. She patted his hand. "I'm going inside to tell Mr. Shapiro you're not feeling too well, okay? Maybe he'll want to call the doctor for you."

As Rosa started to get up, Ike reached for her hand. He pulled her gently back and she sat again. He didn't want management getting involved in this one, thank you very much. But he wouldn't mind trying to get something clear in his mind, now that he had an objective observer to work with.

"Let me ask you something, Rosa." He pointed toward the ocean. "What do you see out there?"

"You mean the water?"

"That, and beyond."

She studied Ike's face for a moment and then came to a decision. What a sweet woman, Ike thought.

"Well, starting here, I see people on the boardwalk, and bicycles, and a girl running. Mrs. Astroth is by the rail feeding the gulls her leftovers from lunch. Then I see the beach, the empty lifeguard stand, the jetties. How am I doing, Ike?"

"Great. What else?"

"Then the waves, and out a ways the water gets smooth. A boat going by. Then the sky, a few clouds that look like maybe cauliflower." She turned to look at Ike. "I've got to go back inside, okay?"

He nodded. "You know what I see, Rosa? I see a haze, mostly. The color of bones, or maybe ashes. Some movement here and there, but mostly haze."

"Well, I know that sometimes happens when you get on in years."

Ike nodded again. "Except everything's looked more or less

like that to me for the last sixty-some years. Ashes and bones. All right, you go back to your desk, Rosa dear. I'm sorry I kept you away. But listen, don't say anything to Mr. Shapiro. I'm all right."

Rosa shook her head and Ike didn't know if that meant she wouldn't mention his little spell or she didn't think he was all right. But then she was gone. He had overstated things there, but not by much. Couldn't see squat anymore. What, he should go for some of this Nazi money and get his eyes fixed? A kind of reverse Nazi medical procedure. That would be ironic, use their money to clear up his vision as though it could correct what he saw in memory now? What did Ike want with money anyway? He had all he needed to continue living at The Golden Sands; Sheldon was fine, and childless; there was nothing Ike wanted to do anymore. Well, maybe he could finance two or three years worth of lunches here so he didn't have to look at any more cream of kohlrabi. Or get in touch with Cantor Bloom's people.

Were the camps just about money, then? Was this some kind of absurd tort settlement? A little moral lapse, we apologize, here's the money we confiscated, with interest, and now we're even, goodbye. It hurt Ike's head to think about this. Right between the eyes, as a matter of fact, and he hated that. But if he didn't go ahead and claim his money, and with most of the survivors dying off now, everybody half-dead all over again, suppose the money just sat there in Switzerland?

Ike sensed a sudden darkening and figured that the cauliflower clouds had thickened to cover the sun. Time to go inside and see what was happening in the Red Room. Or go upstairs and lie down for a while. It was good to have the freedom to decide things like this. Ike would at least acknowledge that much.

He still had his wits about him, unlike Jack Levinsky chasing after what's-her-name.

He entered the lobby and headed for the elevator. When he passed the garbage can near Rosa's desk, he reached into his pocket for the letter. Then he stopped. He remembered the look on his brother-in-law's face that time Ike told him about being an alien in England. Or Molly when she asked about the camps and he refused to talk to her. It was the source of their only real conflict in all those golden fifty years together. Then he remembered, in a terrible rush, face after gaunt face: Mordecai Solly Moishe David Max Zvi Abie Charles Bella Kate Howard, and the sight of bones and ashes, and he took his hands from his pockets, walked to the elevator and pressed the button. He would think of something to do with the money. Even if all he could imagine now was to burn it.

The Tour

Esther Myerson sat in a wheelchair trying to figure out where she was. Straight ahead she saw the ocean, but the air was too cold and the water wasn't green enough for this to be Florida. Looking closer, she saw that the beach was all wrong too. It was short and gray, like a cracked slate patio, with long fingers of rock jutting out into the breakers. Beach! She was in Long Beach, even though the beach was short. She was in the state New York, county of something, the city of Long of Leach of Short—

Esther turned to mention this to her husband, Sonny, but he wasn't there. She looked left and right to see whether Sonny had wandered off along the boardwalk, but he wasn't in sight. That's Sonny to a tee, she thought. When a woman needs to have questions answered, he's gone. Fix the plumbing, move a credenza, the man's right there. Speak, and he disappears.

Sonny will be back, Esther told herself, patting the blanket that was keeping her numb legs warm. He was supposed to inform Esther when he was going somewhere, and when he would return. No, wait a minute, that was their daughter Sandy who was supposed to keep them posted like that. It was all right for Sonny to come and go as he pleased, which he'd been doing since they first met in 1936. In a field in Lakehurst, New Jersey, where she was taking photographs of the first transatlantic dirigible flight. That enormous, doomed zeppelin called the *Hindenburg* settling down against its mooring mast amid bursts of gas. Lighter-than-air flight. Everyone thought it was such a miracle until the *Hindenburg* blew up in the very same field a year later. What had Sonny been doing there? Selling soda, if Esther remembered correctly, and flirting shamelessly. But he'd had such a lighter-than-air way about him.

Saul Myerson had been called Sonny for so long that no one seemed to know his real first name. Including Esther, who was pretty sure she did once know it. Not any more, though, like most things. She reminded herself to ask Sandy next time the girl came to visit. Esther would ask Sonny herself, except he might think it strange that she'd forgotten such a thing. Knowing she'd forget to remember to ask what she'd forgotten, Esther took a small notebook and ballpoint pen out of her purse, flipped to the first page, which was full of scribble, then to the second, and wrote *ask Sonny's name.* She put the pad and pen away. What she most wanted was an old-fashioned fountain pen. But who could find a real pen nowadays, without spending a small fortune? In the old days, when Sonny was off on one of his sales trips through the New England territory, she could ask him to bring back a fountain pen. Esther took her pad and pen back out and wrote *ask Sonny for a fountain pen.*

Now someone was laughing at her. No, it was a gull circling overhead. A door opened behind her and Esther heard footsteps approaching. On the boardwalk, sound traveled oddly. It seemed to be coming up through her chair rather than on waves of air. The waves were frothy there in front of her, and loud. What had she been thinking of? Oh, yes: she could feel people before seeing them. This person coming behind her was tall and dense, so it couldn't be Sonny, but maybe it was Sandy. Except Esther didn't think she was expecting her daughter to visit.

"Hello there, Esther."

A man, but not Sonny, who never called her Esther. *Tootsie*, but not Esther. *Do I look like a Tootsie?* she would ask, feigning anger, and Sonny would let his eyes roam over her body for a moment before answering, each and every time, *A Tea for Tootsie.* Which was, if she remembered right, the name of a candy.

Just a second, now, hadn't someone spoken to her? Esther struggled to turn her head far enough to see, and there was Fred Foreksin. No, Fred Framkin, with his hands in his pockets and that ridiculous baseball cap, Brooklyn Dodgers, a team that didn't even exist anymore, yanked down around his ears. The ears stood out like flippers. Fred Framkin, the chief playboy at the Epstein Retirement Center. *You look splendid today,* he would say, or *You have such gorgeous hair eyes hands whatever.* No matter where she turned during the day, it seemed that Fred Framkin was audible and complimenting what everyone knew was not worth complimenting.

"How are you this afternoon, Esther?"

Had she greeted him? It was too awful, this failure to know what was happening in her life. If you can't remember, Esther thought, you can't think. And if you can't think, you aren't living. Didn't a famous philosopher say something like that? But I am thinking, sort of. Isn't that just what I'm doing now? So I must be living. Not necessarily in the here and now, but living. What a muddle. Hearing Fred's voice now made her remember hearing it earlier today, crooning in the corner of the lobby that so-and-so had such gorgeous skin when the woman's skin looked like melted candlewax.

"I'm fine."

He nodded. "Gorgeous day, no?"

"A little chilly for me."

"But just look at those clouds, like fine threads."

Esther found that she was able to keep up with this conversation, and that simple fact made her willing to continue talking to him. Humor the man. Poor Fred Framkin, lonely and flirting with God, see if that got him anywhere. Ooooo, Esther thought, that was a good one. When she didn't have to be alone with her own head, when she could talk sense to somebody, and think about what somebody else was saying or doing, then it seemed that she could still manage. At least for a few minutes, till she got tired. It was mostly when she found herself on her own and sinking deeper into her mind and memory that things began to fall apart so badly.

Esther nodded. She said, "I've lived in—" and then came to a sudden stop. Where was she, again? Not Florida, any fool could see that. Skip it. She swallowed and began again, "I've lived here for the last—" and stopped again. How long had she and Sonny been here, wherever here was? Twenty years? Who knew, who cared? Where is that man? "You know what I'd like to do on a day like this? Get in a nice warm car and take a tour."

Fred walked away from her wheelchair, touched the railing of the boardwalk with his hand and came back to her, like a man completing a relay race, and said, "So where would you go on this tour of yours? Around Long Beach and back?"

Bless his heart, Esther thought. He didn't say she had a gorgeous anything, but he did tell her what she needed to know. And she knew perfectly well where she was now, Long Beach, out on the boardwalk behind the Epstein Retirement Center, after lunch. "Fire Island. I'd like to see Fire Island, finally. Hidden Hills, the Hamptons, Montauk. All these places I've heard of for years, so beautiful, filled with artists, immense light. I would like to go see them all. Shelter Island, too."

"I got news for you, Esther. They sound a lot better than they look, with their fancy names and their crowds of people."

Another gull chuckled above them, and Esther thought, Good, at least somebody thinks Fred Framkin is funny.

She turned her head to ask him what, exactly, was wrong with those places. But he was gone. What is it with the men around here? Esther wondered. You look away for two seconds and that's it, they've disappeared. Sonny was always like that. Summer of 1937, Esther thought she'd lost him for good. He said he'd gone over to the old country, which was Russia then, but had been Poland when his family lived there. A quick trip to the area around Minsk, he said when he got home, waving one elegant hand in the air to indicate *Over there, behind me,* sounding as if he had only been scouting goods for his new sales territory. What kind of man goes off to Europe and leaves a bride of less-than-a-year behind, not a word from him the whole time he's gone, and then shows up to resume his life like nothing had happened? And what kind of woman stands for it? For sixty-plus years?

She must have dozed for a moment, and was jolted up in her chair when she heard, "There you are!"

Oh wonderful, Esther thought, now the seagulls are starting to sound like my daughter. Just what I need. She was blinded by the sudden autumn light.

Then Sandy Myerson appeared in front of her mother, eclipsing the sun. First glare, then shadow. Esther felt the need to sneeze. Her daughter squatted like she was about to speak with a child, put her arms around Esther and exhaled the slithery odor of French fries before kissing her forehead. "I was worried about you."

"For what, darling? How far could I go?" Esther wasn't sure if she'd said that or just thought it. "Besides, Minh at the front desk knew where I was."

Sandy stood, mumbled "She wasn't there," and moved behind her mother's chair. Releasing the brake, she began wheeling Esther east. What is it with this child? she wondered. Who said I wanted to go anywhere? Tired, chilled, all Esther wanted was a nap and a cup of Lipton's tea. "Lookit, Ma: there's a guy your age going for a swim. Can you believe that? Makes me shiver just to see him in his trunks."

"That's probably your father. He loves his cold-weather swims. I was wondering where he'd gone."

Sandy stopped pushing so abruptly that Esther almost fell out of the chair. The child drives the same way. Esther was surprised her daughter still had a license. "Cut that out, Ma. I hate when you do that."

"What did I do?" She readjusted the blanket. "You're the one who stopped short."

"You know Daddy's dead." Esther heard Sandy ratting around inside her purse, heard her blowing her nose, sniffling. "Today is six months. It's hard enough," she stopped herself there, snorted, snapped her purse shut and resumed pushing Esther's chair in silence.

They reached the boardwalk's end sooner than Esther would have imagined possible. Speeding, of course. I should wear a helmet. Sandy braked the chair beside a bench and sat near Esther gazing east toward land's-end.

"I shouldn't have gotten upset like that," she said. "It's just, you know, today."

Without looking at her, Esther patted Sandy's hands. She had forgotten what they were talking about, but did remember that her daughter had been upset. Still, Esther was proud of herself; she was doing pretty well, considering the time of day. Who could keep track of what Sandy was jabbering about, anyway? There were times when Esther had been in her forties and forgot what the child was saying. No, she wasn't feeling too muddled now. Look at that view. Without any boardwalk in the foreground, the beach seemed to open like a sigh. Even its color seemed brighter, bonier. Maybe they were in Florida after all, or somewhere in between, say Carolina. When she realized that Sandy had been talking, Esther shook her head like a swimmer surfacing from a dive and said, in a voice that sounded oddly like her own mother's, "Pardon me, dear. What were you saying?"

"I asked if there's anything you need, anything you want. We could go for a little drive. Go to a mall. You need pantyhose, makeup?"

Pantyhose? What about stockings? Oh, Lord, Sonny always loved to watch Esther put on her stockings. Maybe even more than he loved watching her take them off. He was always in a bit of a rush, when it got to that part. But while she was dressing he would sit there, his thick lips pursed, a shy smile threatening to break out, those enormous brown eyes transfixed as she stretched each leg up and worked the silk down and hooked it to her garter. Made her feel like Gypsy Rose Lee or somebody. Betty Grable. Esther was hardly a woman to display herself, but in the privacy of their bedroom, what Sonny called their *bood-wahr*, she enjoyed the change that her movements brought over him.

"Or maybe some new shoes," Sandy said, when Esther didn't respond. "That nice store over in Lynbrook."

"You know what I'd like to do? I'd like to drive around Long Island a little. A tour. Could we do that? I need to get out more. It helps me think better. And there are so many places I've wanted to see, right here almost under my nose."

"Are you serious?"

Esther slowly closed her eyes in assent, then opened them to gaze at her daughter's lovely face. A bit pinched with worry just now, but plainly beautiful all the same. Her father's big brown eyes. And fortunately, Esther thought, my own mother's lush blond hair with all that curl. A reasonable Myerson nose, long and curved but not too. Everything casually aligned, no fuss with makeup or clothes. Sandy was a girl you loved to look at, and her response had always been to distract attention by talking. Smart, like me, Esther said to herself, or perhaps said out loud, and quick, like her father. The best thing we ever did.

"Only let's do it tomorrow. I'm tired now. Could you take me back?"

The whole way west along the boardwalk, Sandy questioned her. Wouldn't it be better to do something practical instead of just driving around? They'd done that last week, didn't Esther remember? Did she feel all right, should they go see Dr. Gilbert? Would she be comfortable in the car for such a long time? On and on.

Finally, just before they reached the Epstein, Esther interrupted. "What was the name of that corn meal dish your father loved? You remember, the stuff he used to smear with marinara sauce? I don't know where he learned about that."

"For God's sake, what does that have to do with anything? Are you sure you're okay?"

Esther reached back and took Sandy's hand. She moved it to her lips and said, "I'm fine. Now what was that mush called?"

"Polenta, Ma. Only daddy mispronounced it. 'Plenty,' he called it. He'd say, 'Ahhhh, Tootsie, you always make me good plenty.'"

"That's right. Polenta. Now listen to me, Sandy. If I sit around this place, my brain turns into polenta. I have to get out. It's the only time I can think or make sense of anything."

"I thought you liked it here."

"It's fine here. All I'm asking you is to take me for a drive tomorrow. Can you do that?"

Sandy kissed the top of her mother's head, sighed and began wheeling her into the building. "What time?"

As soon as she got back to her room, Esther took out her pen and pad, and wrote *Sandy. 9:30.* She ripped the page out and placed it next to her bed, by the alarm clock. Then she picked it up and added *Wednesday.*

In the morning, when her alarm went off, Esther saw the note and wondered what Sandy wanted now. Those first few years of her daughter's life, Esther thought she would never get over being tired. Sandy didn't sleep through the night till she was about seven years old, it seemed, and Esther just wore down. Sonny was no help. Gone to service his territory, gone to buy goods, gone for a rest. A rest! The nerve. Still, every time Sonny came back home, Esther felt the same old thrill. Now he was gone again, and Sandy was making first-thing-in-the-morning demands again, and Esther was so fatigued again that she thought she might not be able to get out of bed. What could this be about? They'd had a lovely visit—sometime last week, wasn't it? At her age, Esther had enough trouble sleeping without needing to set an alarm to wake her just when she'd finally sunk deep enough to dream. 9:30 was awfully early in the morning to go anywhere. Esther figured she'd better call right now and get it cleared up.

"You just caught me, Ma. I'm on my way out the door."

"That's okay. You can call me when you get back."

"But I'm coming over to get you. Don't you remember?" Esther hated when people asked her that. Sure, she had a little trouble with her memory now and then, but why was everybody so fixated on it?

"Of course I remember. But I'm feeling fine. I don't need to see the doctor."

"We're not going to the doctor. We're going on a tour."

"A tour? What a lovely idea." She looked around her room, but didn't see any packed suitcases. Her travel clothes weren't hanging on the closet door. What was this child talking about?

"We'll go see the old lighthouse on Fire Island this morning. I've packed a lunch and if you're not too tired we might get back to the bird sanctuary at Tobay Beach. How's that sound?"

"Oh, Sandy, that's absolutely divine. It's so sweet of you to come up with this." Esther was surprised and delighted. You just never knew what this world and what your child would do. Who said that getting old was all a horror? Such kindness, and in such unexpected places. Not all surprises were bad surprises, after all. Esther realized that she hadn't heard Sandy's last few remarks. "Listen, I'd better go shower and eat breakfast if you're going to be here at 9:30. We can talk then."

It was risky to do anything quickly, but Esther rushed through her shower and put on her handiest outfit. No stains on the front, so she figured she hadn't worn it in the last few days. A woman can't allow herself to look shabby, or to be repetitious in her clothing. Even if there weren't many people in the place who would remember what you wore yesterday.

At breakfast, Esther was sitting close enough to Fred Framkin's table to hear him compliment Josephine Klein on her lovely outfit, and Madeline Grosswald on her shoes. Esther was in such a good mood, looking at the note beside her plate which said *Front door, 9:30, the tour,* that she leaned over and said, "Good morning, Fred. That's a gorgeous part you have in your hair."

He stopped talking and looked at her, eyes twitching side to side, unsure if Esther might be mocking him. Fred's mouth hung open, his spoon was poised with a load of milky oatmeal dripping onto the tablecloth, and his huge ears began reddening.

Watching him with a hazy smile on her face, Esther began to worry. Her brows knit and smile faded. She wondered if Fred might be having a stroke. Or was he going to throw his oatmeal at her? And what had she said that might have upset him? Excuse me for saying hello! Come to think of it, what had she said at all?

As she watched, Esther saw Fred reach a decision. He closed and opened his eyes, swallowed, put his spoon down, nodded at her, took a long calming breath and said, "Thank you."

It was as though someone had dropped a tray full of dishes.

No one had dared to return a compliment from Fred, not knowing what he might think or do with such encouragement. Everyone at both tables stopped talking and turned to look at Fred and Esther. Even the busboy froze in his tracks, hand outstretched, a look of confusion on his face. Dazzled by the morning light flooding into the room from two massive windows in the east wall, Esther didn't see the shift in attention, but she sensed it. What a day. *Thank you,* clear as a bell. She leaned back and began to eat.

Fred removed the napkin from his collar. Without looking around, he stood and began circling the table so he could move toward the door. Esther spoke to him without knowing she was about to do it. Just swallowed and said, "Here," handing him the note. *Front door, 9:30, the tour.* Why not? Sandy's car had plenty of room, and the man might enjoy a day out, or something. See? Don't try so hard, Mr. Fred Framkin.

After breakfast, Esther went to her room to freshen up. She flicked on the television as usual, glad for the company of a voice while she did her business. Then, tired from having missed the extra sleep, she sat on her bed for a moment to rest. The ringing phone jolted her from sleep.

"Mrs. Myerson, this Minh downstairs."

Esther nodded.

"You okay, Mrs. Myerson?"

"Oh, yes, thank you dear. I'm glad you called."

"Your daughter here. She say you supposed meet her for some kind of tour. Out front. She double-parked."

Esther took the elevator down, straightening her clothes a bit and pleased at what the word "tour" brought to mind. That Sandy was such a darling, such a fine daughter. It was always wonderful to travel with her, even just on day-trips, because Sandy was an eager, avid road companion. Once when they accompanied Sonny to New England, Sandy had been too excited to sleep at night in the hotels. She would whisper to herself, narrating the story of the day, the sound of her voice slowly putting Esther and Sonny to sleep. But when they got back home, Sandy immediately came down with the mumps, or maybe that was the time she got the measles. The flu, that's what it was.

When the elevator door opened, Sandy was waiting for her. They kissed, Sandy saying, "There you are," and headed toward the sunshine. "Ma, I think you ought to have a cell phone so I can keep in touch better. Or a beeper. No, that wouldn't work. Cell phone, that's the answer."

Esther had no idea what the child was babbling about. Or what she was doing in the lobby. "I thought you had to stay in the car because it's double-parked."

"Your friend Mr. Framkin is watching it for me."

"Oh, that's very nice of him. Did he compliment you on your car?"

"Said it was gorgeous. He's got his Mets hat on and he's all ready to go with us."

Esther stopped walking. She looked at Sandy and said, "You invited Fred Framkin to come with us? Oh, I don't know, he'll talk such nonsense all day. I hope we're not going far."

Sandy said, "You—" and then stopped herself. She took a deep breath and said, "Next stop, Fire Island."

When they were settled in their seats, Sandy let the car idle for a moment while she collected her thoughts. There was only so much a person could do before the chaos took over. There really was no fighting it. She drove east toward Meadowbrook Parkway, adjusting the heat, making sure Esther was comfortable in the front and Fred in the back. "Isn't it nice to get out?"

"Oh, yes," Esther said. "I'm so happy. Such a grand idea you had! Now tell me, where are we going?"

Sandy looked in her rear view mirror to find Fred Framkin's eyes trained on her beneath the yanked-down visor of his hat. The expression on his face was neutral, she thought, the lines around his mouth accentuating a frown that could only be habitual because his eyes were gleaming.

"The old lighthouse on Fire Island, Ma. We're not allowed to drive on the island, but we can park there and go see inside."

"Fire Island? Oh, I've always wanted to go there. Thank you so much, darling."

Let Us Rejoice!

Norma Corman felt reconciled to her illness. It was only the symptoms that bothered her. Tremors, for instance. Her arm waving over the bingo board like a magic wand, forked meat flitting before her mouth like a bumblebee, handwriting like code, head forever nodding Yes. She thought it made her seem simple and stupid, though the only thing she had left was her fine mind. And now look: tea everywhere.

All these humiliations Norma could do without. Along with the half-hour it took to button a blouse or the endless waiting for her legs to listen to her brain and get moving. Terrible, the way her mind would race ahead and her dwindling body dawdle behind. Time was all messed up now. She was older? She was sick? Fine! But for heaven's sake why did she have to look like a jittering puppet?

"Don't be so hard on yourself," her son Arnold kept telling her. "It's barely noticeable."

Barely noticeable? Arnold's moustache was barely noticeable; Norma's tremors were a spectacle. They were checked skirts with striped sweaters. They were shocking pink. Or worse: riveting as a river of blood.

Norma hoped her son was more honest and understanding with his patients than with his mother. Your tumor that fills up the entire x-ray is barely noticeable, Mr. Applebaum. The scar from where we removed your jawbone is barely noticeable, Mrs. Dorfman. A radiologist who barely notices his mother vibrating like an unbalanced clothes dryer doesn't inspire confidence.

Get hold of yourself, Norma Corman! She repeated this like a mantra. The worst thing for her was stress, was agitation, and here she was already in a frenzy over nothing. And nodding like a ninny while sloshing Lipton's over poor Mr. Herschel Birnbaum's poplin bingo-playing jacket.

e⌒

With all his famous son's money, Herschel could go buy himself another poplin jacket. As soon as Norma thought that, she felt terrible. Unkind thoughts. Another symptom, maybe. She considered reaching over with her wad of Kleenex to dab at Herschel's stain, but was afraid of where her hand might land.

He turned to her and whispered, with a sense of dark wonder in his abrasive voice. Something like, "I can't believe it." He didn't seem to be talking about the tea, though. Going on, as usual, full of childhood memories. He didn't need a tea stain to set him off. "How could it happen?"

A few weeks ago, Herschel had learned that his son the clothier had an inoperable brain tumor. This wasn't the way it was supposed to work, he kept saying. Young people were supposed to keep going along. Especially, to Herschel's way of thinking, rich young people. Illness, if it struck a young person, was only for the poor. But mostly illness was for the old. Herschel was supposed to get the tumors, the heart attack, the stroke. It was wrong, that's all. And a man like Herschel's son Bruce, still single, no heir, all that money and what did it get him? No, Herschel just couldn't understand how it could happen to Bruce.

Norma couldn't help herself, but she was sure she understood how it could happen to Bruce—or anyone. Didn't something similar happen to her own husband when he was too young for it to happen to him? A common enough story, the young nowadays, their lifestyles, the unhealthy air and unhealthy habits. She wouldn't be surprised if soon there were more old people on the planet than young ones. Why, no one would . . . Where was she, Norma wondered? Yes, right, Herschel sitting there next to her and staring at his stained jacket. His poor son. Norma thought about his misfortune now whenever she saw Herschel Birnbaum, and this disappointed her. But there it was, obsessive and circuitous thought, like another kind of tremor, and she knew by now she couldn't fight these things.

Behind Herschel's back, residents of the Jacobson Care Home fell into discussing what he should do for his son before the poor young man passed away. Also what they would do with so little time but so much money. See every show on Broadway. Move to Israel. Send the son to one of those *goyishe* miracle places, Lourdes or Knock or one of the other Catholic shrines. Donate. Cancer research, or heart stroke Alzheimer's. Build the Bruce Birnbaum Wing on the Jacobson Care Home where food would taste like real food and where the long-term residents who were there when Herschel went through his awful loss would get to live with him. On and on. Norma kept silent, but since she nodded at every suggestion, no one pressed her to reveal her own thoughts. They assumed she agreed with theirs.

But Norma knew they'd go crazy if she told them what her plan really was. In fact, it was coming together as a true plan, not some fantasy like all the rest. She thought she might talk about her brainstorm seriously, intimately, with Herschel, sometime soon. Let him know how much it meant to her, how good it would be for him and for Bruce to have a project like this to work on, and see what he had to say. About bringing Harry Belafonte to the Jacobson for one of their Saturday night entertainment programs.

The business about time being messed up was sometimes worse for Norma than all the rest of her symptoms put together. When her son Arnold walked into the lobby to visit her, he looked so much older than his own father that Norma got very confused. Of course, at fifty-six Arnold was older than his father ever was. Poor Ed, dead at forty-one, collapsed among the hats in his shop.

What Norma remembered most about Ed Corman now was how much he hated being a haberdasher. She could no longer remember how he sounded, his squeaky bedroom whisper, his whining, not even his lovely singing voice, a tenor that he hoped would bring him success on the stage. She couldn't call to mind his body, his face, his eyes. Just the top of his head, where Ed was always directing Norma to look as he tried on and took off hats. That, and his sulking despair, and his hatred for the work he did. Hats instead of songs! The man endured his work because he believed a thriving business would enable his son to be a brain surgeon. Which it might have, if the business ever thrived as heartily as Ed imagined, or if Arnold had been dedicated enough, smart enough, dexterous enough. Well, they hadn't done too badly, though the Cormans' success may have been on a less lofty scale than Ed had hoped. Norma knew how grief had worked on her husband and she knew in her heart it was good that Ed hadn't lived to see the way things turned out. The gloom that always shadowed their home, and the lamentation that was becoming their life's soundtrack, would have rendered him—rendered them—desolate.

Well, what could be done about any of it now? Besides, the life Norma had lived these last four decades had been devoted to expiation, to acceptance. To moving ahead. Or, as she sometimes told herself, to the light. She had supported Arnold in his belated maturation and had seen him into a thriving radiology practice. She had taught fifth-grade English. She had become a serious person.

1959, that was when everything had collapsed. Ed dropped dead, Arnold dropped out, and Norma dropped in for a brief visit to Paradise. Where, as she remembered almost every day since, she'd made a complete fool of herself.

Though she was still sitting beside Herschel Birnbaum and still studying the stain on his jacket, hearing him carry on about *it makes no sense,* and though she was still aware of her mind working out the best way to approach Herschel about inviting Harry Belafonte to the Jacobson Care Home, of seducing the glum fellow into it any way she could, Norma also knew that she was about to time-travel again. She thought the time-travel might have something to do with those long spaces between thought and action that were an increasing part of her Parkinson's progression. An erasure of time's borderlines, or a gorge in the landscape of her brain into which she sometimes toppled. Time-travel was memory at its most porous. Her body here, her mind there, everything disconnected. Even Norma's tremors stopped when she traveled like this.

A wind-blown morning, late winter, 1959. Norma had been reading the Sunday *Times* when she noticed an ad: *Harry Belafonte, Live in Concert at Carnegie Hall.* Two benefit shows, April 19 and 20. She must have uttered some sudden sound because Ed put the sports section down and looked at her. Or rather, wrinkled his brow at her. She could remember the silence of those Sunday mornings in Baldwin, the belching of bulldozers halted till Monday at 8:00, reading with Ed in the living room, Arnold out somewhere.

"What?" Ed had asked.

Norma forced her eyes away from the Belafonte photo in the paper and said, "More coffee?"

But Ed was back to reading about spring training. Mickey Mantle and his pre-season knees, Yogi Berra and his ongoing streak of errorless games, Bill Veeck buying the White Sox. Norma breathed deeply, slowing her pulse rate, letting herself look back at the paper.

Of course Harry Belafonte was a beautiful man, maybe the most beautiful man Norma had ever seen. But that wasn't, she felt, what drew her to him. She was not and never had been one of those women who had intimate fantasies about celebrities. About anyone, really. Norma Corman was no bobby-soxer. Sinatra? Wonderful singer, but she never imagined herself in bed with that scrawny, big-eared, womanizing bully. Perry Como, Vic Damone, Julius LaRosa? Absurd. Her own husband sang as well as Julius LaRosa. Belafonte's passion stirred her, of course it did, and his righteousness, his dignity, his commitment to causes. These two

concerts were benefits for schools! She respected him. And look
how he loved his Caribbean roots, his people, how he yearned.
That was part of it, the yearning. Which was in his body and in his
sensuous movements when he sang, in his way with a melody. He
kindled joy in her. All right, all right, he was sexy, he was exotic,
the whole package. Probably could cook, too. But the truth was,
Harry Belafonte's voice, so soft, so full of breath, a top-to-bottom
kind of voice, with a moist touch, just sparked something in her.
Norma could no more explain it than she could dowse the sudden
fire—there was no other word for it—that Harry Belafonte lit in
her . . . she was going to say *in her soul* but it was really in her guts,
her *kishkes*. That was not something Ed Corman did for her, not
even when he sang in the shower.

So she would have to get a ticket and see Harry Belafonte at
Carnegie Hall. Not with Ed, though. When she'd asked him last year
what he thought about Harry Belafonte, her husband had scratched
his bald spot and said, "Is he still playing for the Red Sox?" Typical
of the discussions they had been having for the last few years. And
she couldn't go with Arnold, who might have gone with her to see
Chuck Berry or Jerry Lee Lewis, but hardly Harry Belafonte.

She bought two tickets without knowing who would use the
other. Ordered them the next morning and found herself luxu-
riating in the power that the extra ticket seemed to give her. On
whom would Norma bestow the honor of attending the concert?
Then she wondered if she could go alone. Keep it all to herself.
Maybe, but it would be easier to explain her actions to Ed if she
were going with a friend.

Only after five other friends had turned her down, all amid
startled laughter, had Irene Rogovin agreed to travel into the city

with Norma. Irene Rogovin. Norma, scanning the room at the Jacobson Care Home without registering anything she saw, let the name tumble down the rapids of her memory. She hadn't thought of Irene in almost forty years. And God forgive her, Norma can remember feeling huge relief when she heard that Irene had run off to Phoenix with that man she met playing bridge. When would that have been? Winter of 1961? Right around the time of Kennedy's inauguration because Norma remembered listening to that speech, and drifting into joyful thoughts about being freed of Irene at last. The only witness to Norma's humiliation, vanished to the hinterlands!

The evening of the Belafonte concert had started so well. Norma wore her new mauve blouse and a black skirt with that fashionably slim line. She wore pearls. And Irene was ready on time, all in blue, yakking about the hijacked flight from Havana as she walked toward the car. Such a splendid city for a honeymoon, Irene said. Poor Batista and his men, all facing certain death. No wonder they had fled. What would happen next? People would have to start honeymooning in St. Thomas, or something.

They parked at the commuter station. Train, with almost no one aboard to crowd them, was there in an instant. Lobster Cantonese at Ruby Foo's that Norma could only nibble in her excitement. At Carnegie Hall, their seats were close enough to the stage so she could see clearly, and the man who sat in front of her was so short that he didn't obstruct the least glimpse of Harry's body.

As the overture began, Norma could barely contain herself. She swore she could see Harry's eye glitter through a peephole in the curtain. He was looking her way, she was sure of it. He came out singing "Wake Up, Wake Up, Darlin' Cora," and Norma rose in her seat. She didn't know what had happened, or that anything unusual had taken place, till she felt Irene's hand pressing down on her shoulder as though to keep her from sailing away like a balloon. Norma patted Irene's hand in return, knowing that Harry's voice made a woman want to touch and be touched.

When he sang "John Henry," Norma couldn't help herself. It made her weep. So heroic, so compassionate! And she hadn't realized that she knew the lyrics to so many of his songs. Not just "Day-O" and "Jamaica Farewell" and "Mama Look a Boo Boo," which anybody might know by heart, but the old standards too, "Cotton Fields" and "The Marching Saints." Had anyone ever sung them this well? *Oh Lord, I want to be in that number.* It was as though Norma and Harry had known each other forever.

"Sit down," someone hissed. Irene had her hand on Norma again.

Yes, *the sun shines daily on the mountain top!* Norma pressed her hands together and tucked them under her chin as though in prayer.

The tether snapped when Harry began to sing "Hava Nageela." *Let Us Rejoice!* His voice down low, his magenta silk shirt open down low, his black slacks tight as he swayed, a flash in his smile, his eyes smiling right at Norma, it was as though he were telling her, by singing in Hebrew, that he was for her. He was one with her. She stood, shook free of Irene's hand. He was slowly, steadily increasing the song's tempo. She was smiling back, telling him that she understood. She was in motion then, coming to him, coming to the light, answering his call.

$\backsim$

Norma felt that it was never too late to atone. Her letters of apology had gone unanswered and by the start of 1960 she realized that Harry must never have seen them. His staff or someone close to him had disposed of them. May not have opened any after reading the first one. Another crank. Then she thought that he wouldn't, of course, remember her, maybe not remember the whole episode. One among many, she supposed. But Norma never forgot. Not her shame, and not the exhilaration that preceded it. She dreamed about having made it all the way into Harry's arms, about having rushed into the spotlight only to find herself stark naked, about running across the stage toward Harry with one of Ed's hats extended from her hand as an offering. It was terrible and it never went away, the memory vivid as a car wreck, still there even as her brain ossified under the onslaught of Parkinson's. Though Norma's memory in its tyranny often played tricks on her, this one great humiliation never wavered in its thick, detailed presence. April 1959, Norma radiant with joy, her blouse unbuttoned to match Harry's opened shirt, her arms wide, stumbling up the stage steps at Carnegie Hall screaming *Hava na ra na na!* like a possessed person, an utter imbecile.

Beside her now, Herschel Birnbaum was turning his head and bringing Norma back from 1959. A blink of the eye and forty-two years were breached.

"I let him down," Herschel said. "Just like I let everyone down."

She thought about reaching out to him, offering Herschel what was in her hand so that he could begin cleaning himself up, but the pull wasn't strong enough. She wasn't ready to come back to the present, to the new millennium, to Herschel Birnbaum and his poplin jacket and his dying son. Not yet. Besides, he didn't seem to have registered the stain. She had noticed here that some people are just always lost in their own thoughts.

What had it been, two months later? End of June, 1959, and Ed was gone. Norma remembered how upset he had been over the U.S. Senate's refusal to approve Lewis L. Strauss as Secretary of Commerce. He was in a rage the night it happened, saying that it was a travesty, that Eisenhower was entitled to have the man he wanted to run Commerce, that business would suffer, no cabinet appointment had been blocked since 1925, and who cares if Strauss lied a little bit about the problems of radiation fallout when he was running the Atomic Energy Commission. A little radiation, big deal! We got radiation when we went to the doctor, to the dentist, we got radiation when we had our feet x-rayed at the shoe store. So what? Ed was apoplectic, and Norma just sat there at the dining room table and watched him turn crimson, knowing his anger wasn't about Congress or Lewis Strauss but about Norma and Harry Belafonte. Stored up over the last two months, it finally erupted.

She'd told Ed back in April, what else could she do, and it was as though she had confessed to adultery instead of to public embarrassment. Which, she knew in her heart, wasn't far off. That first night, he yelled and threatened, then he gave her the silent treatment. He wouldn't touch her, wouldn't look at her, wouldn't even eat the beef and pork meat loaf she cooked for him because it was his absolute favorite. For two months, nothing else was said. Then, over the appointment of Lewis L. Strauss, over another dinner he wouldn't eat, he blew up.

The next morning at his shop, Ed died. Just like that, a massive heart attack, face down on the counter in a jumble of fedoras.

Norma believed then, and she never stopped believing, that it had been her fault. She'd killed him with her shame and her joy and her momentary wildness, aspects of her deepest self that she withheld from Ed but gave to Harry Belafonte.

Within another three months, Arnold was gone too. He had been so depressed in February, when Buddy Holly, Ritchie Valens, and the Big Bopper died in a plane crash. Then Chuck Berry got in trouble in St. Louis, bringing a young girl up from Mexico, just as Jerry Lee Lewis had gotten in trouble for marrying his young cousin. And Elvis was in the Army. Arnold saw the arrival of Frankie Avalon and Bobby Rydell as the death of his beloved music, and he saw "American Bandstand" as its funeral service, so he bolted. At least that was how he explained it to his mother in a disjointed letter mailed a month later from Amsterdam. Norma never stopped believing that this, too, had been her fault. Arnold's flight from home—from America—wasn't about music. It was about Ed's death, which was Norma's doing and was, in its way, more about music than Arnold's disappearance was. The whole matter was too circular and too confusing for Norma, but she couldn't stop thinking about it.

She shut her eyes. Norma wasn't surprised that the instantaneous passage of forty-two years left her dizzy, which is why she always shut her eyes. Opening them, she saw that Herschel Birnbaum was looking at her with something like compassion in his eyes.

"I'm sorry, Herschel."

"I'm sorry too."

She nodded, looking at him. At times like this, the tremors could actually be useful, making it seem as though she sweetly accepted his apology while she tried to figure out what the hell was going on. Why was Herschel apologizing to her? Norma saw that he was serious. This wasn't some kind of tease.

"What are you sorry about?" she asked.

"For dominating the conversation, of course. I've been babbling." He looked down. "Again." He looked even further down, and seemed in danger of sliding off his chair. "Ever since I got the news, I can't seem to shut up about it. So please forgive me, yes?"

Norma nodded some more. The man was obviously having a spell or something. Not that she could blame him, under the circumstances. She had heard nothing from him in all this time, in all these forty-two years she had just lived through over again. There was too much of this going on at the Jacobson Care Home, too many of them lapsing into senility. Poor Herschel. Then it occurred to Norma that he might be telling her the truth, or rather, the truth as it pertained to what was happening here and now. Had he been talking all this time, thinking she was paying attention?

Why, Norma wondered, did people have to be living so long nowadays? What was the point here?

"I think," Herschel whispered, "that you and I may have reached critical mass." He gazed at her. "You know what critical mass is?" Seeing her acknowledgment, he went on: "The suffering now, it just goes on and on. Constant. It's like a nuclear chain reaction. I could see it in your eyes the whole time I was telling you about poor Bruce. You've had your losses too, all you can bear, and now the sadness is without end. Am I right?"

Norma all of a sudden felt her attention lock into place. This required great care. Here was Herschel Birnbaum, the man grieving for his dying son, the least happy man she had ever met, implying that her losses and his losses bound them together in pain. Or was it guilt? Lord, she must have looked awful there, a few minutes ago, a few decades ago. Who was Norma Corman to share grief with Herschel Birnbaum? And what was this about sadness without end? Yes, this required care.

In recent years, Norma had learned how to catch up on conversations that she'd drifted away from. It didn't take much. "Tell me more," she said, and as she knew he would, Herschel started all over again.

The grandfather's tumors erupting like a ring of mushrooms after a summer storm. The grandmother with the rotten insides. In the mother's family, too, cancer of the this and cancer of the that, lesions, explosions in the glands and bowels and blood. Even though nobody smoked, nobody drank too much, nobody ate bacon or the other non-kosher killer foods, nobody lived in toxic territories. Norma had heard these before, but this time she listened. Herschel was tormented by having survived, that much she understood right away. By escaping the family legacy of growths and metastases. Now Herschel was talking about smears and scopes and taps and biopsies and images and tests. Chemo and radiation.

"Nothing to be done," Herschel muttered. "Nothing to be done."

"But there's always something to be done, Herschel. There's prayer. There are miracles. Plus, it's never too late to atone." Where did that come from? Oh, right, she had been saying the same thing to herself for years.

As she sat there nodding, Norma felt a sudden surge of happiness. Joy, almost. It was good to listen to Herschel. She could ignore that sandpaper voice of his and learn to pay attention. He was, of all things, a nice man! He cared, at least about some things, about certain human things, if you could get past the irritation in his voice and in his repetitive, labyrinthine tales and lists of symptoms.

"He knows you love him," Norma said, not exactly sure to whom she was referring, but confident anyway that it was the right thing to say.

Herschel lifted his head, watery eyes finding her face. He seemed to be assessing her with new interest, as though he too had finally heard something she'd said. "I suppose."

"And besides, at the end, who knows anything anyway?"

Norma stopped because Herschel's face seemed to be blurring, softening in some way she didn't understand. He seemed to be transforming right before her eyes. Growing younger, darkening. Oh, wonderful, Norma thought. If he turns into Harry Belafonte, then I know I'm hopeless. Wouldn't it be wonderful if this late-life traveling through time gave us the chance to make things right? Because what is aging but an occasion for letting go, for shedding not just density and clarity but the whole freight of blame and grief and loss? Freight, Norma thought. What am I, a choo-choo train? If only she could forget. Lose her mind the way she was losing her body, the way so many of the people around here were losing their minds. Uncouple everything and shut down the engine as the journey ends in one slowing drift toward home. *Toot toot!* Well, she couldn't, it appeared, forget. But from here, maybe she could look back afresh. Catch a glimpse of all that freight as it rolled away behind her.

Without knowing what she would say, but determined not to mention trains, Norma started talking again. "The end is just a lot of faces staring down at you while you pass away. Or they say now that you rise up, and look down at the top of their heads but you also see their faces looking down at you. Very frightening idea, I think."

⟡

There he was now, someone younger let loose from within the older Herschel. Handsome, yes, but there was more to it. He was full of life again, vital. She could look at him forever, if he would only stay like this. His gaze was level, boring into her, with a smile in there somewhere. Norma could tell that this fine man was pleased to be sitting with her, listening to what she was saying even if it made almost no sense. And she was pleased too. What was going on here, romance? A glimmer of something like it, anyway. Imagine.

"What?" Herschel whispered.

"I'm sorry," Norma said. But it was less an apology than a cry of release. She had the feeling that Herschel would gladly give her anything she wanted, including Harry Belafonte. Then she realized how wrong she'd been. How self-absorbed. If she and Herschel were united in anything, it was in not being responsible for everything they'd always held themselves responsible for. She hadn't killed Ed. If blame for her husband's death was to be placed anywhere, place it on Ed's own hatred of being a haberdasher or his failed dreams or his flawed genes. Besides, he might still be alive inside her, and no longer troubled about Carnegie Hall. She hadn't banished Arnold to Amsterdam, either, nor had she caused him to be a radiologist instead of a brain surgeon. He went where he wanted and did what he wanted, always. That was, in fact, what was good about her son. His contrariness, his independence. In

Arnold Corman, guilt and blame were barely noticeable.

"It's all right," Norma said. "It really is." She reached out to Herschel, the wadded Kleenex in her hand like a flower, and it looked beautiful as it fluttered toward him on an invisible wind.

THE SHOREFRONT MANOR

Lunch was Belle Wilbur's favorite time of day. She sat on the maroon velvet couch in the lobby until precisely eight minutes past noon, when the other residents of the retirement home were seated in the dining room but not yet starting to eat their fruit compotes. Then she rose to enter arm-in-arm with her ninety-seven-year-old boyfriend Lou Goetz. Too bad Lou, who had not yet agreed to be called Louis, was now so bent and twisted that he was shorter than Belle. It would be nice to have him towering over her, a handsome knight with his Belle of the Ball. But at least he still kept his head up.

They strolled toward the rear of the dining room, where windows opened out to a view of the sea. It was a view to be prized. Belle twisted her torso slightly to the left and then slightly to the right as they passed the other tables, flicking her fingers at them like the Pope in procession. She knew just what the girls were thinking about, how jealous they were.

So what if Lou Goetz hadn't quite come back from his last stroke and had a somewhat limited vocabulary. So what if he used a cane, which Belle would have to get him to replace with something a little more elegant than that aluminum pharmacy-bought model. Something hand-carved, maybe in hazel or oak. Meanwhile, just have a peek at the man's thick white mane, his notched and dignified nose, those burly hands.

But look, there at the table next to Belle and Lou's, the table reserved for residents with guests, was that ridiculous Ava Ravel with her raven-black hair in ringlets, sitting like a princess beside her son the engineer. A man goes to school for twenty years to learn how to use a slide-rule? Pathetic. Ava was waving back at Belle with her face shattered, to be perfectly frank, simply shattered by an obnoxious smile.

Belle was suddenly aware of the clinking of spoons against glass bowls and false teeth. She could barely bring herself to sit there, let alone eat. But of course she smiled and inclined her head in Ava's direction. This was the same woman who insisted on announcing each stop an elevator made, like the place was a damned department store, and who read the activities board aloud to anyone in the vicinity. Ava had the nerve to gloat?

And of course here comes Rhoda Brown over to the table to meet the brilliant Mr. Ravel, her eyes aflutter. What's she going to do, ask him for a measurement?

Belle was startled by the appearance of a waiter over her shoulder. He put down a basket of rolls and she had to restrain herself from slapping his hand, which came entirely too close to her body. This particular waiter had started to work last week, and spoke a language which apparently had no words for *the food you're serving me is vile,* which made him impossible to properly insult. They charge her $2,500 a month and give her slops for lunch.

Don't they know who she is?

"How can you manage to eat?" Belle hissed at Lou, leaning close enough for him to hear.

He turned his milky blue eyes toward her, held the spoon poised above his prunes, and said what he always said when Belle asked him a direct question: "Sputnik."

After lunch, when Belle was safely back in her room and even before she had gone to the bathroom, she telephoned her son in California. It was 10:00 there. The lazy lump should be awake.

When Zachary answered, Belle got right to the point. "I want you should visit me. It's been four years since you last saw your mother."

"Ma, you know I can't do that. I'm sick."

"You're sick? All month, I've had such a pain in the side my doctor thinks I should have my gall bladder out."

"You already had it removed. October, 1983."

"Well, it grew back. Now stop arguing and tell me when you can come."

"We've been over this, remember? I can't come there. If you want to see me, you need to come here. I have to get dialysis three days a week. Actually four, starting today."

"So get your dialysis here. New York has better equipment anyway. Or skip a week. It wouldn't hurt you."

With Zachary, there was always something. First he was too busy, then he had gout, then he had diabetes, then he was blind, now he had dialysis. Belle didn't know why he was like this. So he wasn't a doctor, a lawyer, a movie producer, even an engineer. She'd tried not to let that bother her. So he was a cockamamie inventor of little plastic things for computers that someone was always patenting just before him. Let him invent a way to have dialysis here, the big shot.

"I'll pay for your trip, Zachary dear, if that's it."

"That's not it, Ma." She could hear his deep, calming inhalation just like that father of his, may he rest in peace. Abner? Aaron? Always with the deep breaths like he was about to expire from frustration. Zachary should be so lucky as to have had a father like Louis Goetz. Who, by the way, should have changed that last name to Gray or Green.

"So if it's not money, what is it, Zachary? What is it?"

"Listen, I have to go. My cab'll be here in ten minutes and it takes at least that long for me to get downstairs. Okay?"

"So go already." Belle had to get downstairs too, for God's sake. Lou was waiting in the card room. "So sorry to bother you."

"No bother, Ma. I just have to go." Then he coughed that fake cough of his and said, "You know, you really should come to California. And before much longer. Say in the next two months."

Of all the nerve! Here Belle was calling to tell her son he should visit her and he ends up turning it around, now she should visit him. Mistake, right from the start. What could she have been thinking? It was just that awful scene at lunch. But the girls were all so dotty they'd have forgotten about Ava Ravel and her son by dinnertime anyway. No need to bring Zachary all the way to New York. He'd end up staying a whole week, she'd have to take care of him again like when he was a child. Such a clingy one, that Zachary, and now in her advancing years he wants her to come all the way across country so he can cling some more, just when she was free at last.

"You know I can't travel anymore," Belle said.

Now he was saying something about two months again, like he hadn't heard a thing she'd said. "That's what the doctor told me, Ma. I've got two months, max."

"All right," she said. "When it's over, then you can come see me. Now I have to hang up."

Fine, Belle thought as she shut the door behind her, two months. The girls will be so jealous. Louis on the right, Zachary on the left. I'll be the envy of the entire place.

The Wanderer

Once Norman Hertz walked through the peeling wooden door, he forgot the door had been there. This was the genius of his getaway. He never worried about what was behind him. Stopped against a swollen threshold, never quite shutting, the door blocked the late autumn breeze and kept Norm's secret. He'd been gone almost an hour before anyone noticed.

At ninety-two, his chest was curled inward as though the heart of him had never really wanted to go where the rest of him might be headed. But otherwise, he looked strong and healthy enough. White hair gathered in tight coils around a small, freckled clearing where his yarmulke would go if the new aide, Sonia, had remembered to pin it on that morning. His face had a focused look without a crinkle of humor in it, a mask of determined strength. His fists were clenched. You might not feel the need to get out of Norm's way when he walked, but you wouldn't be drawn to helping him either.

All Norm knew was that he had to get out of that place where they'd been confining him. Even when he was out, he still wanted to get out. Blinking, feeling caged despite the fresh air on his skin, he headed east toward the sun, toward the ocean that was three thousand miles away.

e⌐

Sonia trotted back down the hall and stopped outside the social worker's office to catch her breath. She was thirty-two, built like a whippet, had gone six days now without smoking and thought she'd finally gotten that new start. So this was not good. Definitely not the way to end her first week on this job.

She leaned her head and shoulders into the social work office, coughed once in the direction of her boss, and said, "I think he's gone."

"Who's gone?" Jennifer Yellin initialed a weekly assessment form before looking up. *Ah, the new girl. Something with an S. Sally? Shawna? It'll come to me.*

"The old man in 24."

"There are two old men in 24, Sonia." *All right!* Jennifer thought: *Sonia. So I've still got a functioning brain.* Sometimes she wondered if memory loss were contagious. But no, she knew it was overwork that explained her lapses. Overwork, or it could be menopause, which had kidnapped the real Jennifer about a year ago, and streaked her black hair with two gray stripes. "There's Abe Solway in 24 and also Norman Hertz."

"The white-haired one."

Jennifer sighed. "They both have white hair."

Sonia sucked in her gut, hunched her shoulders and raised her chin. "He's built like a question mark, you know?"

"That'd be Norm. Okay, now what do you mean by *Gone?* Where's he gone to? Did you check the bathroom? Sometimes he forgets to get up off the toilet."

"That's just it. I checked everywhere, and then I asked Raul to check too. He's still looking."

Uh-oh. Trying to control her alarm, Jennifer walked past Sonia into the hall and looked both ways. The front door, which led into the nursing home lobby, was shut. Back door, the one that sometimes got stuck, was open, but that was because Raul was standing in it. Looming there, actually. Filling the thing. He came back inside and pulled the door shut. He saw Jennifer and shrugged, palms up in front of his chest.

Without looking back at Sonia, speaking very slowly, Jennifer said, "Tell me about it."

Sonia said, "Well," and burst into tears.

e

Norman Hertz. Jennifer liked him, even though he didn't say much, because he had a lovely smile. Sure, sometimes it was hard to tell when he was smiling versus when he was grimacing, but it thawed his frozen expression in ways that made Jennifer feel what it might be like to have been loved by this man.

As she walked through the facility, opening and closing various doors, moving equipment, she tried to remember all she knew about Norm. It was better than thinking about Sonia and her mini-breakdown. Just what Jennifer needed—staff hysterics at a time like this. Then she stopped and put her hand to her mouth. *Oh God, what's happening to me? I'm a social worker. I'm supposed to*

support people when they dissolve in hysterics. I'm empathetic and caring.
She shook her head and started moving again.

Jennifer's files hadn't been much help in suggesting where
Norm might have gone. Most of the material there was typical
intake information about health status, insurance, age, medications,
advance directives. At the time of admission, Norm's son hadn't
provided anything in the way of background, and there was noth-
ing new in the file, no life story. There hadn't been any photo-
graphs in Norm's room either.

Jennifer knew they needed to do a better job about collecting
patient historical detail. But most patients had such severe memo-
ry impairment that their lives were almost lost to them. And most
of the families were too busy with their own lives, or too absorbed
in the trauma of relocating a demented parent, to sit down and
chat about the past.

Norm was, if she remembered right, from Germany. The son
had once stopped Jennifer in the hall and invited her to sit in the
common room with them. He'd talked for about forty-five sec-
onds, then got up to leave, which explained why he'd waylaid Jen-
nifer. The old man was a partisan during the war, something like
that. He'd fled Germany, but gone in the wrong direction. That's
what the son said, all in one rush. It was coming back to her now.
Ended up in western Russia, Poland, in the woods somewhere,
fighting the Nazis along with other Jews. Daring acts of sabotage.
Or maybe she was mixing in some of what she'd read in novels.
Primo Levi? Whatever, she now had the picture of Norm as a
young man in the wintry woods, wandering wherever the cause
took him. No home, no place of stillness. And now, ninety-two
and somewhere in the middle stages of probable Alzheimer's, he

seemed to be reverting to old behaviors. On the move, stealthy, acting as his younger self had acted. Or not. Jennifer knew that wandering was often an Alzheimer's symptom. Best not to make too much metaphoric meaning out of what was essentially an organic behavior. Did she really know this man? After almost two years here, he was after all still a case, his past and character as scattered in Jennifer's mind as it must have been in his own.

Norm himself would say nothing about his life. He'd just walk the halls. Whenever he noticed Jennifer in his path or sitting in her office, which wasn't often even though she was often there, Norm would stop and reach for her hand.

"Will you walk with me?"

She liked that. She tried to walk with him at least once every day, even taking him outside for a brief stroll if she had the time.

Now, as though Norm were everywhere she was looking but yet nowhere, she kept hearing his voice. *Will you walk with me?*

℮

Norm stopped for red lights, though he wasn't aware of them. People stood nearby. No one took special notice of the old man. The land sloped gently downhill. After a half-hour of walking straight, he saw water. Sunlight winking off the surface. It was a river, though. Not the ocean. He was not smelling seawater.

When the street curved, Norm was suddenly able to see trees looming above the shops and low-rise condos. A hillside, dotted with houses, rising into the unmistakable dark mass of woods. Evergreen, mostly. As far as he could see to the north, those woods kept going.

Good. Now he knew where he was. The old haunts. Once inside the woods, he would be able to find the camp. Norm waited for the light to turn green, crossed the street and headed north. Woods. Norm knew the woods, and he knew where he needed to go.

$\mathcal{e}$

"He can't have gone far," Jennifer said. She'd been into corners of the building she never knew existed. She'd also seen staff she'd never seen before, and a gorgeous oil painting of a pushcart that had been donated by one of Portland's premier artists. Some day, she would have to take a real tour. Now, though, she was in the main office and distracted by a winking of lights on the most elaborate telephone system she'd ever seen. "We've had everybody looking."

The Administrator nodded. He picked up his coffee mug and blew into it, but his breath came back into his face. Empty. He put the mug down and tried to remember what he knew about this old man, Norman Hertz. A wanderer, of course. The more active ones sometimes get to that stage. Which is why we lock the unit. Damn it, should have had that back door fixed already. More budget cuts, more deferred expenditures, more patient problems: the cycle never seems to reverse itself. Pretty soon it'll be an open zoo around here. He realized that Jennifer was waiting for him to say something. Since he didn't remember what she'd said last, he muttered his usual "And so?"

"Well, Raul and a couple of the guys from the kitchen fanned out through the neighborhood. Maybe they've had more luck."

The Administrator nodded. Luck. No, he didn't think so. There wasn't much luck to be found around here these days. He'd been meaning to look over the emergency procedures. But damn it, he'd only been Administrator for six weeks. Other priorities. Best to wait till the staff finished their neighborhood search before panicking. Guy's probably lost and walking in circles. Or someone found him, took him inside for a cup of coffee. Be nice to have a cup of coffee right about now. That's it, Mr. Hertz is probably doing just fine and we'll get a call here pretty soon from the Good Samaritan who took him in. At least it wasn't winter yet.

"His son stopped visiting a couple months ago," Jennifer said, since the Administrator was just staring at her. "We see that happen over and over. One day, after a visit, he just said, 'What's the point? He doesn't know I'm here.' Hasn't been back since. Calls once a week. But maybe Norm did know when his son was here, you know? And now maybe he decided to go visit his son since his son wasn't visiting him."

The Administrator shrugged. *Don't want to call the son just yet. No no. Let's see what our guys find first. Hertz, Norman. There was a daughter too, wasn't there? Or was that Eli Brody, the one they had in 24 before Hertz moved in? Hertz. Right, now he remembered. The son's a contractor. Worked on that project for the city, the new stadium. Successful kid. Nice looking wife, drives a Lexus. No, wait, that's the grandson. The son's the one who looks just like the old man. Insurance? No, real estate. Yeah, son's a developer.* He shrugged again.

"Norm never tried to get out before," Jennifer said. "Just walked the hall all day. Up one side and down the other. I'd see him go by every few minutes."

Raul knocked on the Administrator's door. He was panting

and looking deeply distressed. He held up an index finger. *Gimme a minute.*

Oh great, we've got a patient missing and now an aide is going to croak. Someone should tell this Raul to go on a diet. Nice enough looking guy, very adept with the patients, teases the old ladies, listens to the old men. Good person to have around. We don't need him having a stroke on us.

"No sign of Norm," Raul finally said.

So. The Administrator picked up his coffee cup again and put it down. Call the cops first, then the grandson.

Raul and Sonia sat in the staff lounge. He'd liked the way Sonia looked from Day One, but they hadn't had time to talk. Besides, the home seemed to encourage a culture of disengagement among its staff. Aides might chatter with other aides, social workers with social workers, maintenance with maintenance, but there were lines that did not get crossed. Raul still had to look at name tags in order to figure out who was who, and he knew that it was not acceptable behavior to be glancing at people's chests before addressing them. Now with this crisis, and with Sonia so upset, he was glad he'd bided his time before breaking the ice with her.

"So where's he from?"

"Germany, I think." Sonia pushed her straw in and out of the ice in her drink. "That's what Jennifer told me just now."

"No, I mean where did he live before he came to the nursing home?"

"Southeast Portland. I remember the grandson's wife said he

came from over by the college."

"Well then." Raul nodded and started to lean back in the chair, which creaked in alarm. So he sat forward, trying not to crowd Sonia, and said, "That's probably where he's headed."

"That's like five, six miles. With lots of traffic. And a river to cross."

"Still."

"He can't remember where the dining room is. How's he going to remember how to get to his old home?"

Raul knew. Sometimes, these old people had more going on up there than we realized. His own mother, dead now four years, spent her last few months trying to get to the little corner market.

"Let me tell you something," he said. "In her last years, my mother thought I was my father. She thought the visiting nurse was my sister and the mailman was my uncle Alex. But she knew exactly where the market was, the place she worked half her life. Up the hill by this path that was invisible unless you knew where it was, across three lanes of traffic, then through those streets that go like a maze through Ladd's Edition. I come home at midnight to an empty house, I know just the route to take to track my mother down."

Sonia nodded. The story didn't surprise her anymore, even though she'd only been working here for a week. But it made her sad anyway. Maybe because she was hearing it from a guy who hadn't spoken two words to her before. It's all or nothing around here, she thought.

"I feel like it's my fault," Sonia said, lifting her glass and returning it to the table without drinking. "I should've been paying better attention."

Raul reached across and patted her hand. "No way you can

watch them all. That's something I know. Anybody's fault, it's Miss Social Worker there in her office. Or the Administrator who didn't pay attention when I told him three times already that the door wouldn't shut all the time. Or it's the old man's son for putting him here. The old man himself for living too long."

"Nobody lives past fifty-three in my family," Sonia said. Then, as though hearing a tape of what she'd just spoken aloud, she opened her eyes wide and put her hands over her chest.

e

Norm came to a bridge. The street had been steep for a while now, and he knew he was getting close to the woods. But he kept having to stop to catch his breath. Halfway across the bridge, as he leaned against the railing, Norm felt that the whole world was opening up. He noticed that the buildings on both sides had disappeared, and he felt the unimpeded wind across his body.

This had been quite a march, but he knew marching. He was more than a little tired, but all that walking in the halls had kept him fit and he was doing what he was trained to do. He was heading back to the woods, back to camp. And there it was, to his left and down below the bridge. A narrowing path into the heart of a forest. And lookit, someone was running right into it, a little guy in a torn shirt and shorts even in this cold weather. Norm understood what that was like. How many times had he made his getaway in whatever clothes he could scrounge, or in the tattered remains of what he'd been wearing before they caught him, or before some blast had nearly stripped him naked.

Norm turned around and made his way back to the foot of

this bridge, where he saw a crude wooden staircase that led underneath. He'd bet there was a river or a creek or some kind of water down there, and some remnants of shelter. He'd be just fine. He went down the stairs. The running man was gone, but Norm saw there was only one place he could've entered the forest.

ℯ

The Administrator paged Jennifer. She'd assembled the other residents of the locked unit and had been discussing—if that was what you could call it—how they felt about Norm and his recent behavior. She returned his call from the common room where they all sat nibbling cookies and looking at the photograph Jennifer had brought to help them think about Norm.

"The police are checking all through the neighborhood," the Administrator said. "Also across the river there, where the patient resided before moving to the home."

Jennifer put a finger in her ear to block out the noise coming from an agitated Abe Solway, who kept repeating a two-note call, *Norm Norm,* at the top of his lungs. Abe was just being helpful, and trying to convince his roommate to come out of the television where he was convinced Norm was hiding.

"I'm sure they'll find him, then."

The Administrator shrugged. He was making a note to himself: *Call the son at 1:00 if not found.* When he didn't speak, Jennifer asked him if there was anything else he wanted her to do.

"Look, are you free?" he asked. "Because I'd like to come down to your office and look at what you've got."

"Sure, come on." The Administrator hadn't visited Jennifer's office so far. In fact, she wasn't sure he'd ever left his own office since he took the job. "Though you've seen everything I have in my files on Norman Hertz."

"Thanks. I'll be there in about eight minutes."

Sonia put her arm around Abe Solway and led him away from the television. She turned a chair so it faced the bank of windows opposite, and Abe sat his bulk down with a deep sigh.

She hadn't really looked at him before. It was hard enough remembering the basics about each resident on the unit, and there hadn't been a chance or reason to spend much personal time with them. Abe Solway, she remembered now, had suffered a stroke and was experiencing some additional, minor obstructive events. He had trouble talking, but one look at him told Sonia that his mind was working more clearly than his speech or his body. Must be awful torture. Here she was, with a body that worked almost too well, a smoothly operating machine she never had to think about, but after one week on this job she realized her mind was over-whelmed. She'd speak gobbledegook in the staff lounge, asking Raul to pass her the magnet when she meant the magazine, telling Jennifer in a meeting that the woman in 18 had an accident in pu-bic instead of in public. Maybe, she thought, it was time to reserve a room here for herself. Anyway, it made her see this Abe Solway differently. See him, period. And she was starting to understand why a Norm Hertz might bolt.

"How do you feel, Mr. Solway?"

"Hanh?"

"You all right? Anything you need?"

The old man nodded firmly, but didn't speak.

℮

"What's he like?" the Administrator asked. He was looking over Jennifer's shoulder, so she turned around to see who he was talking about. There was a picture of her husband there, on top of her filing cabinet, where she'd stashed it when her desk got too crowded.

"Jeff? He's solid. Works at the city planning office."

The Administrator shook his head. "I thought his name was Norm. Norman J. Hertz. Jeff—is that what the J stands for?"

Jennifer took a long, slow breath. Maybe, she thought, being out of his office makes the man lose his grip. "Sorry, I got confused. Let's see: Norm's middle name is Julius. Jeff is my husband. But I forgot what you asked."

The Administrator shrugged. He'd forgotten too. He took off his glasses, gave his face a vigorous rub, and said what was on his mind. "No sign of our Mr. Hertz so far. The police called his son and his grandson, which was too bad because I was hoping not to bother them. I was going to call them myself, of course, when it seemed necessary. Now they're angry at us for losing the old man and for failing to call them right away. They're also angry at the police, and they've all hopped in their cars and gone looking for Poppa. What a mess."

"I heard it on the radio too."

"Oh God."

"Yeah, a report, a description of Norm. It's kinda gone public on us."

The Administrator stood up. "Jennifer," he said, and stopped. He sat back down, said "Jennifer" again, then got up and left her office.

"Hey!" She realized that she wasn't sure what to call the Administrator. No one else seemed to be, either.

He leaned back so that only his head appeared in Jennifer's doorway. His eyebrows were raised, brow furrowed, and he was looking at Jeff's picture again. "Hey? You said hey?"

Now it was Jennifer's turn to shrug.

"You could call me Dan. I wish somebody would."

❧

It would be getting dark soon. They were all together now in the staff lounge with the television on for the early news. There on the screen, nearly life-size, was Norm's face, looking younger and more animated than he was now, and then a picture of the nursing home, looking newer and less ramshackle than it was now. Must've doctored the shot, the Administrator thought. Leave it to the media.

For the past hour, Jennifer, Sonia, and Raul, along with the two daytime nurses on the unit and the Administrator, had been brainstorming. That's what the Administrator called it. Sonia and Raul hadn't even considered going home when their shifts ended. Jennifer and the Administrator, whom she was still trying to imagine calling Dan, hadn't eaten since breakfast. Hours ago, they'd lost track of time, lost the need to parcel out blame, and stopped writing Talking Points on the chalkboard.

They sat in a circle, trying to remember anything and everything that might give them a clue to Norm's whereabouts. He hadn't yet shown up at his old house or his son's house or his grandson's house. He wasn't anywhere in the neighborhood. He hadn't ridden in a taxi. He wasn't in any of the hospitals.

Then, before actually seeing anyone arrive, they all felt the air in the lounge change. One by one they turned to face the door. As though having waited for all movement to stop first, Aaron Hertz entered the room.

Norm's son looked enough like the old man to confuse them at first. He's back! Rejuvenated by his escapade, his hair was gray instead of white and there was a bit more of it. His spine was straight again, so that he was a few inches taller and wider. But no. They saw soon enough that it was the developer Aaron Hertz and he seemed to be expanding as they watched, reddening, trembling.

"How the fuck do you lose a demented old man?"

The Administrator stood. He held both hands out as though to fend off an attack, though Hertz had stopped in the doorway. "Yes, yes, welcome, welcome. We're very glad you're here, Mr. Hertz. We were just talking about your father."

"Talking! What good is talking?"

"Well." The Administrator's breath seemed to be constricting as he spoke. "The police are conducting their search. And we were hoping to help. As we have helped all day. Trying to probe deeper. You might say. Understand your father's needs. Suggest where he might have gone."

"A bit late for that, isn't it?" Hertz refused to enter the room any further. It seemed to Jennifer that he was afraid he might attack them all if he got within reach. Raul shifted his chair so that he could intercept Hertz if the need arose.

The Administrator coughed and said, "Tell us, Mr. Hertz, what was your father like?"

"What was he like? You see him every day, you stupid son-of-a-bitch, you know what he was like: He was like a zombie."

"Is," Jennifer whispered. "Not was."

There was movement behind Hertz, who turned sideways to let his son pass. Louis Hertz floated past Aaron and into the room. He'd been named after his grandmother Louisa, Norm's beloved wife, to whom he bore a striking resemblance, and his first gestures were exactly those his grandmother would have used in this situation. He smiled. He bobbed his head. He scratched his neck. He urged everyone to sit, put his hand on his father's shoulder, put a finger to his lips. "Easy, Pop. Easy now."

"They want to know what your grandfather's like. Isn't that wonderful? Maybe if they figure out he's a zombie, they'll conclude he couldn't have disappeared because zombies are easy to find, and we can all go home. Idiots."

"Any room in the circle?" Louis asked. "Come on, Pop, let's see what happens. Can't be any worse than driving the streets trying to spot Grandpa."

℮

Norm found the trail and followed a small creek. There was a ruined stone hut where the trail intersected another, larger trail that twisted uphill. He looked inside the hut. Rubble, weeds, trash.

Norm knew it must've been bombed by the Nazis. No one was there. He needed a rest, so he settled down on the dirt floor with his sore back against the one remaining wall. He was tired. The light was failing. It was getting cold. There should be someone here beside him, Norm knew that. Little fellow from Vilnius, never would tell anybody his name. Called him Nat because he was small and annoying as a gnat. Handy with explosives. An engineer before the *Einsatzgruppen* had come through and eliminated his village. He'll be back in a minute. Out scavenging. Norm felt like the exhaustion and the ache in his bones would never go away. But, as Nat had told him, you could never relax, never sleep all the way down to where your soul might get some rest, because the Nazis were everywhere. Everywhere. Every. Where?

When he first heard footsteps, Nat was unable to move. He'd been asleep for a few minutes, and now wasn't sure where he was. Not far from the Russian border, maybe. The footsteps neared, heading back the way Norm had come. Nat? No, he could hear voices now. Women. He'd be all right, then. There was still some light, and the women were hurrying. He forced himself to stand. He moved out of the hut, into the light, and the women stopped. In a moment, having seen that he was very old and very ragged, they came closer.

"Are you all right?" the taller one said.

"Wait, he's the man who wandered away from that old folks home," her friend whispered. "How'd he get all the way over here?"

Not liking the whisper, he began backing into the hut. They both reached out to him.

"You're Norm, right? Norm something. Don't worry, we'll help you."

They were all right, Norm thought. Their touch was kind.

"Will you walk with me?" he said.

$\mathcal{C}\curvearrowright$

It was dark now, but no one had left the staff lounge. One of the nightshift aides had brought them coffee, then a box of crackers she'd found in the snack room.

Jennifer had spoken first, describing Norm's pacing of the hallways, his disdain of most activities except bingo, his apparent affection for Abe Solway. She remembered the time Norm, moved to tears, had come to find her because Abe had soiled his pants and would not get up off the floor of their room. Sonia spoke briefly, apologizing over and over for failing to check on the door. She took Norm's yarmulke out of her pocket and held it up, apologizing for yet another failure. She also may have failed to be sure his socks matched, but wasn't certain. Raul said Norm was so amazingly strong it was hard to get the old man to do anything he didn't want to do. And the hands on that old man: they were huge, they were powerful. Raul wasn't confident he could've whipped Norm in a fair fight, back in the old days. When Raul finished, everyone from the nursing home looked over at Louis so he began to reminisce. Sitting on his grandfather's knee hearing stories of Poland from when Poland was really Poland. Drives into the mountains to see waterfalls. Hikes in the woods. More hikes in the woods.

"He's not dead!" Aaron interrupted. "Damn it, Louis, stop talking like he's dead."

There was a long pause then. Sonia started to cry, so Jennifer reached over and took the younger woman's hand. Raul grabbed

Sonia's other hand and, without thinking about it, Jennifer responded by reaching for the Administrator's hand.

"Dan," she said. "What about you?"

No one knew who she was talking to. The Administrator shrugged, and reached for Louis's hand. Louis turned in his chair to reach for his father's hand, but Aaron recoiled.

At that point, several cell phones rang. Before anyone answered, Jennifer knew. She looked over at Louis, still twisted around in his chair, his hand in mid-air, his face confused as he waited for his father to narrow the distance between them. The woods, Jennifer thought. Of course. She started to laugh, but it emerged more like a sob.

II

THE ROYAL FAMILY

Saturday mornings always smelled like meat. When Milton Webb woke his son Danny in the dark, an odor of raw pork was already on his hands.

One hand was spread across Danny's brow, the thumb and pinky squeezing his temples in a steady massage. Danny's eyes fluttered open. It never occurred to him that his father was a small man. Everything about Milton Webb seemed large. He spoke in salvos and his whisper was like the eye of a hurricane. Danny could hear him breathing anywhere in the apartment. Milt had corded, hairy arms and fingers that were so thick he had trouble buttoning shirts. His nose, smashed twice by falling chicken coops, sheered his shadowed face toward the jutting jaw and seemed stretched to a point by its own weight. His huge belly didn't jiggle when he walked. He would make Danny punch him there as hard as he could and would never flinch.

Even when his father stood near Rocco, Danny didn't think of him as small. It just seemed that Rocco, who was some kind of bodyguard at an Italian restaurant and his father's best friend, was a giant. Maybe Rocco would show up at the market today.

Milt was dressed for work, wearing black corduroys and a maroon flannel shirt that didn't show blood. His socks sagged into boots he wouldn't tie until leaving the apartment. Their lace tips clicked on the linoleum when he walked.

"C'mon, pal, it's past time to get up. Now what's the slogan?"

"Kill or be killed," Danny mumbled.

"Right you are. And don't forget, Mr. Alfred J. Honts, who used to be my friend Alf, will gladly take every one of my customers if I'm not careful."

"Except the Chinese restaurants."

"Except the Chinese, right. That's another thing to remember. Your uncle Joseph wanted no part of the Chinese trade, which is why he's selling hats today. Makes me laugh."

Danny turned his head away and gazed at the map hung on his wall. A huge red oval seemed to glow down at him. Ask him to find any volcano in the Ring of Fire and Danny would jab a finger right to it on the map. From Chile up to Alaska and down from Siberia to New Zealand, he could place more than six hundred of the world's most furious mountains. Someday, he promised himself, he would walk within the Valley of Ten Thousand Smokes. He would visit Burney and Barren Island, Tarawera and Ulawun, Purace, Mount St. Helens. He loved just saying their names.

"Uncle Joe's a hatdasher, right?"

"Haberdasher." Milt rolled Danny's head back away from the wall. "Now let's get moving, we open at five."

ॐ

Danny's clothes were in a tall chest that was backed into his closet. He found a pair of dungarees with their cuffs still rolled properly. His father got furious when cuffs were too high or uneven, when they sagged against his sneakers, when they had fade marks. Danny's mother always unrolled the cuffs when she did the wash. He wished she'd leave them alone, since it was so hard to get the cuffs right again, but he didn't have the nerve to ask her. She got enraged when he asked questions about her housekeeping and would scream *Just like your father!*

He slipped on a sweatshirt the same shade of blue as his dungarees. He thought his father might appreciate the match. If so, then this could be his market uniform from now on. Then his father would take him along more Saturdays, like he used to. Danny hoped he might have finally figured out the right thing to do.

Before leaving the room, Danny checked to be sure he hadn't disturbed his brother. Ricky slept on his back with his bad eye half open, so it was difficult to be sure.

Saturdays, Ricky had to meet all morning with his tutor. He hadn't been allowed to go to the market since failing Algebra and History.

Ricky's bad eye had been bad since before Danny was born, so he knew it couldn't be his fault. Something about a broken lens, glass in Ricky's eye, one entire summer of surgeries. Danny dreamed about it sometimes, seeing their father's fist, with its black hairs standing sharp and tall as spikes, make Ricky's glasses explode in his face.

Ricky was asleep. Danny could tell by checking whether the bad eye moved.

He could remember to call him Rick when his brother was awake, but Danny still thought of him as Ricky. It had only been a few weeks since Ricky demanded the name change. Every time Danny forgot, his brother would punch him on the arm. There was a big bruise now on his biceps, but Danny hadn't told his mother the truth about how he'd gotten it. Ricky said that if he did, it would cost Danny his leg.

Danny had trouble keeping up with Ricky's names. Not too long ago, he had a long struggle replacing Richie with Ricky. Now he had to remember Rick.

He checked himself out in the mirror behind their door. Everything looked neat enough, but you could never be sure. He wiped the residue of a sleepstring from the corner of his eye.

Whenever Danny dressed to visit his grandparents, or for Sunday dinner at Lundy's, his father made him go back to his room to change shirts. Shirt selection was his real problem, all right. No matter which one he chose, Danny's first selection was always wrong.

He kept hoping Saturday mornings would be different. As he checked his sweatshirt one more time for cleanliness and color, he thought he might be getting the knack of dressing right.

e͡

Milton Webb flung open the furrowed gray doors of his poultry market. They rumbled in their tracks like subway traincars and disappeared.

"Wake up and fly right!"

Webb's Live Poultry flapped wildly in the coops that lined one wall. As they screamed back at him, their cries ricocheted through the air.

"Help! Help!"

Danny stared at the faces of three scales, which threw dawn light back onto him. The market's floors were covered with fresh sawdust spread last night by his father's helper, a grizzled old man named Gabe.

Soon, Danny knew, the floors would be patched with clots of feathers and blood. He would feel their lumps under his soles all day. There would also be more meat smell. It would remind him of breakfast and make him want to skip lunch. But he couldn't refuse to eat Saturday lunch with his father. That got him madder than anything.

Besides, his father said Danny would get used to the smell. Used to the racket from the coops, too. But it hadn't happened yet.

He stood on the tracks listening to the birds go crazy. His father hurried to the plucking room for aprons. Danny watched him move, the massive shoulders rolling through the air as though he were swimming.

Suddenly, out of the darkness behind him, two hands folded themselves around Danny's face. He was yanked backwards, feet off the ground like a fryer being snatched from its coop, and his head struck something solid. He sank into a heavy stench of offal.

"Ayyyyy, little Milt! Guess who?"

Danny squirmed in the iron grip of his father's helper. Gabriel Kozey once told Danny his hands were so strong because he'd been pulling feathers out of freshly killed birds for forty years.

"You think they wanna come outta there, the plumages?" Gabe had laughed. "It's like jerking out a lady's eyelashes, you know what I mean?"

Danny hated to have Gabe's hands on him. The hands were

mottled with blank blotches, scaly sections paler than the rest and hairless. Probably from all the blood and featherjuice, which Danny could imagine staining like acid.

He thought Gabe must never wash his hands right, the way Milt had taught Danny. He'd bet Gabe didn't flush toilets with his feet, either. He smelled even worse than liver.

No wonder Gabe never got invited home for dinner. Danny liked to imagine his father sending Gabe away from the table to wash better, then his mother checking to make sure Gabe had cleaned the sink after himself. She would probably throw the napkin he used into the incinerator when Gabe left.

Before letting him go, Gabe rolled Danny's head a few times across his belt buckle. Then he nudged him toward the coops and headed back to the plucking room to find Milt.

Danny approached the coops. The chickens crowded into the far corners.

"It's just me. I won't hurt you."

They kept backing up, bunching together and beginning to cry out. Danny stuck a finger in to attract them.

"Here girls."

"Help!" they squawked.

"GET INNA THE OFFICE!" Milt yelled from behind him. Danny hadn't heard him coming. "How many times I gotta tell you keep your hands to yourself? Here, home, everywhere. The hell am I gonna do with you, anyway?

He threw an apron over Danny's head. Despite the fresh soap, he could still smell old blood on it.

"Now don't touch anything." He drew a knife from some place beneath his apron. "You want to lose a finger, here, I'll chop it off for you."

Danny put his hands in his pants pockets. "I'm sorry."

The office was small and warm. The squat cash register filled most of the table. Above it was a shelf that held the old radio. Danny didn't like hearing it talk about the new H-Bomb, so he climbed onto the table and turned the dial until he found a song he knew. *Hey there, you with the stars in your eyes.* His mother could play that one on the piano. He climbed back down. There was a chair on wheels with a flattened cushion sheathed in old aprons. Danny sat in the chair, wheeled it over to the damp window, and wiped a circle clear to watch his father getting the market ready.

First, Milt reached back to slide his hand under the apron and draw out a small plaid flask. He took a deep drink, replaced the flask, and rubbed his arms hard to warm up. Next, he tested the scales. He swept the entryway and put out a fresh roll of brown paper to wrap the dead chickens in. Finally, he lit a cigar, first biting off its tip and screwing on the brown plastic holder that was the same color as the floor of the market.

The last time Danny had been here, it was mid-morning when things started going wrong. He remembered his father glaring at him from in front of the coops. By noon, Milt had called Faye to come down on the bus and get Danny out of there. When his mother arrived, Danny had burst into tears.

Now, Danny wanted to stay out of trouble. At home last Sunday, he'd gotten his father so angry that Milt had kicked his ass like a football. Danny had landed on his knees against the bed. His mother had quickly come over to smooth out the wrinkles and lead Danny out of the room.

Now Milt yanked open the door to a coop. He snatched a capon's feet and swept him face-down through the gate. Wrists snapping, arms flapping faster than wings, he wrapped the legs above the spurs with wire and dangled the capon from the scale's hook.

"Four pounds six," he called over his shoulder.

An old customer, who looked like Grandmother Webb, shrugged her shoulders. She looked over toward the office, where Danny peered back at her.

"Why not?" she said.

Milt produced the knife from under his apron and cut the capon's neck. He took it back to Gabe and then returned to talk to the woman.

Danny came out of the office to watch Gabe thrust the bird, squawking blood, legs kicking air, slit neck first into a can to die. Gabe turned to the plucking machine. He removed a pullet he'd been cleaning for someone who said she'd pick it up at ten.

He addressed Danny without looking at him, as though they'd been chatting all morning. "So, you gonna be a lawyer when you grow up?"

"I don't know." Danny couldn't stop watching the capon's legs. "Maybe."

"A doctor?"

The bird let out a weird rattle and was still. "I don't think so."

"Right, too much school." Gabe put the capon into the plucker and turned the machine on. Danny stood on his toes to watch the feathers fly. "You like school?"

"Can I take him out to my dad?"

"This is an it, not a him." He lifted the carcass and brushed it vigorously. "But sure, do it."

He ripped paper from the fat roll and wrapped the capon quickly. Danny carried the spotted package, taped shut, back to the office. Milt came in to ring the sale.

"Nice job," he said, patting Danny on the head.

When Milt left to hand the package over to the old woman, Danny ran a hand through his hair to check for featherjuice.

⌐

Danny didn't see anything special about the man. It was just before noon when he sauntered in, hands in his jacket pockets, and smiled an anteater's jagged smile.

Milt jerked a thumb over his shoulder like an umpire signaling an out. The man, dressed in a gray overcoat and a hat with one long gray feather, nodded and walked back toward the plucking room.

Gabe burst out of the room at once, as though ejected. He wiped his hands on a towel strung through his apron string, then hurried to the front. He whispered something to Milt, who shook his head.

Danny watched his father come toward the office. Milt's face was drawn tight. Danny took a few steps back from the office door until he reached the wall, wondering what he'd done wrong. He hadn't been letting his nose touch the glass, hadn't spoken, hadn't handled anything (Except the radio! Milt would hear the music!).

Milt stuck his head into the office, but didn't enter. "Stay put," he hissed. "I'm going out back for a while."

Danny was so relieved he wasn't the cause of his father's anger that he couldn't ask any questions. Milt went to where the stranger was waiting, brushed by him without a word, and disappeared.

Danny didn't know Gabe was allowed to wait on customers. He worried that people wouldn't want to buy anything from a man who looked so gory. If a customer came, Danny thought he'd better go out and keep an eye on things.

No one did, though. Gabe stood outside in the morning sun, eyes shut and head tilted skyward. Soon Remo Santselmo, the man who owned the meat market next door, walked over to Gabe, who accepted the proffered flask and drank as deeply as Milt had earlier.

It was still cool, despite the growing brightness. Gabe offered Mr. Santselmo a Lucky Strike.

Danny hung back in the shadows of the coops, watching the men pass the time. Mr. Santselmo, who always traded sausage for chicken with Milt on Friday nights, seemed angry.

"*Criminale,*" he muttered. "Let's talk about something else, hah? We don't gotta talk about those bastards."

"Sure, sure. What about the World Series? You ever see anything like that catch?"

"Ahhh, Willie Mays, you know he's gonna do good. It's a Dusty Rhodes outta nowhere wins you the Series."

"Pitching. Indians give us twenty-one runs in four games. You and me coulda won it, we don't need no Willie Mays. And we got Antonelli on the mound, carried us the whole year."

"The hell with it. I like Brooklyn next year anyhow." Mr. Santselmo threw his cigarette down and stomped on it. "How much longer's Milt gonna put up with this? Makes me embarrassed I'm Italian, even. Goddam."

"Milt's tough."

"That don't make no difference. We're all tough. I'm tough. I been tough since Brooklyn was still a city. Hell, now you can't make no money at all. You gotta keep giving to these people more all the time."

A woman entering Mr. Santselmo's market brought the conversation to a stop. Gabe watched him leave, then turned around and saw Danny standing there. He looked over the boy's shoulder and frowned. Danny understood. He went back into the office and stood as far from the door as he could.

e

Later that evening, Danny watched from the floor of their bedroom as his parents dressed for a costume party. It was his mother's annual Cousins' Club meeting, a tradition every Halloween weekend. He stayed out of their way, but listened to everything they said. The air was filled with the scent of Old Spice and rye whiskey.

"What's Red going as this year?" Milt asked. It was his father's mild voice, the one Danny hadn't heard since first thing in the morning.

"Oh, you know Red. My brother wouldn't tell me the truth if I begged him."

"Probably doesn't even know, himself. I bet you his Commie wife plans their whole life."

"Sasha's no Communist. What's wrong with you? She's simply a nice rich girl from Scarsdale. You know that perfectly well."

"Got a name like a Cossack is all I know. Whispers all the

time, like she's got something to hide."

Last year, Danny remembered, they'd dressed as gangsters. Milt had worn an overcoat and hat like the man who'd come to the market. He'd carried a bottle of liquor under his arm. Danny had thought they'd decided not to wear costumes, but his mother explained that his father was pretending to be Al Capone and she, with a fox stole around her neck and rolling pin in her hand, was his moll.

This year, Danny thought the costumes were much better. His father had a moustache painted on and wore a gold satiny cape that matched his painted cardboard crown. He looked like some movie star King. Faye had made a Queen costume for herself out of sky blue material seasoned with sequins.

"We're The Royal Family," she said.

"Right," Milt grumbled. "King Tut and his wife Nut."

All day, she'd been practicing her Queen Dance. She showed Danny the routine, putting her hands together above her head, shutting her eyes, and bobbing like a turtle going in and out of its shell. Her eyes were encased in black triangles that matched her thickened lips.

"You're doing your head wrong," Milt said.

"What do you know about it?"

"I know that your head should go side to side."

"Mr. King of Egypt, the dance expert."

"I've seen it done right, if that's what you mean. Seen it lots of times."

She turned away from Milt and spoke to Danny. "Your father, whose idea of world travel is a weekend at Lake George, is going to tell me about foreign culture. This is a man who thinks Picasso is some kind of flower."

"Drop it," Milt said. "What do I care if your damn cousins think you're a turtle."

Danny kept playing with his baseball cards on the floor. He had them spread into a field between his parents' beds. Using a pencil for bat and penny for ball, he conducted a full nine-inning game, announcing each at-bat to himself in Red Barber's Mississippi accent.

He liked to be near his parents as they prepared to go out, even if they argued. He'd have to fight back tears when the gray-haired babysitter arrived from the sixth floor and made him go out into the living room.

"Who's better, Dad? Johnny Antonelli or Johnny Podres?"

"Podres. No doubt about it. I mean, Antonelli's Italian."

"Mr. Santselmo thinks Antonelli won the pennant for the Giants last year. I heard him tell Gabe."

"Well, Mr. Santselmo doesn't know anything about anything. Not baseball, not business, and certainly not life. He's as bad as Alf Honts, but at least he sells sausage instead of poultry."

"Who was that man who came in today, when you had to leave? I didn't like him."

Milt looked over at Faye, who was watching them in the mirror. He spoke to her, not Danny, when he said, "Guy who used to be my friend."

"Now what is he?"

"He told me today he's the future. Now go answer the door, pal. Mrs. Auer's here."

Devoted to You

I've never gotten over the Everly Brothers' breakup. It's been on my mind for fifteen years.

Phil and Don were Harmony. I can't hear someone talk about dreams without hearing the Brothers sing. Listen to the way their voices blend. They stood for euphony, pure symmetry. They had the ideal sound for the kind of songs they sang, songs about faith in love. *You know that it's sincere.*

That's fact, not sentiment. They were high tenors, a third of a note difference between them. Lots of guys have the sound together, but Phil and Don had Brotherhood. This wasn't just genetics.

Then came Friday the thirteenth, 1973. The Watergate summer. *Bye-bye love.*

Family was a big deal in America that year. *All in the Family, The Waltons, Sanford and Son* ran 1–2–3 in the Nielsens. The whole country was saying the same thing: pull together, we'll get through this. The President may be failing us, but we've still got the family.

The Everly Brothers were playing the John Wayne Theater at Knott's Berry Farm. Visions of America the Beautiful, and then

116

Phil threw his guitar down and stomped off the stage.

It's hard to sing perfect harmony up there alone. Poor Don. But Phil was *gone gone gone.* So Don gave his "The Everly Brothers Are Dead" speech. I was there in the audience watching this performance.

Truth is, I've got a brother myself. We do not carry a tune. There is no purity when our voices start mingling.

℮↷

Two months before that 1973 concert, I called to invite him. It was May, but you have to get on Lyle's calendar way in advance.

Lyle's always travelling. He sells exotic pelts of some sort, does import/export. To hear him talk, his territory must be the entire western hemisphere.

He won't tell me what kind of animals he gets his pelts from. Says I couldn't afford to buy one, so I shouldn't worry. Truth is, Lyle knows how I feel about killing animals for their skins, which he blames on my college education. This is one of the sore points.

I invited him to the Everly Brothers concert at Knott's Berry Farm. Tickets weren't cheap, but who said anything about paying me back? I was twenty-six years old, working on my doctorate in medieval history, not exactly socking away money in mutual funds. But it was going to be my treat, I made that clear. It'll be fun, I said. Like the old days, when we went to rock 'n' roll shows at the Paramount.

He said he'd call me back. There was someone on the other line.

Two days later, he called me back. I was already asleep. He

knows when I go to bed. Johnny Carson finishes his monologue, I walk upstairs. I've done that since before Carson moved to California and Lyle knows it. When Lyle was still living at home and we shared a room, I'd go to sleep ten, ten-thirty every night. He had the TV on, he talked on the phone, had a couple of his coughing fits, it didn't matter. Eleven the latest, my lights are out.

But when he wants to irritate me, Lyle calls around midnight. First thing he says is, "Oh did I wake you? It's still pretty early here."

He's a bird dog.

"No, Lyle, you didn't wake me. I had to get up to answer the phone."

"So what is it with the Everly Brothers? You still listen to that fifties crap? Nostalgia's bad for you, little brother."

Get this. I was trying to invite the guy to a concert, I'd pay his ticket, fly across the continent to go with him, he had to drive maybe ten minutes to get there, and he criticized my taste in music, my philosophical outlook.

What next, he's going to bill me for his time?

"Lyle, you just don't follow rock 'n' roll anymore, that's all. It's less than five years since the Brothers' last big album. *Roots.* You know what was on that disc? Only 'Shady Grove,' only 'I Wonder if I Care as Much,' done right this time. Lots of people say 'I Wonder' is the best song they ever made."

I knew he'd stopped listening after I said "Lyle." Maybe he heard me say "rock," but by "'n' roll" I knew he was *gone gone gone* himself.

When I stopped for breath, Lyle said, "No originality. Freaks, that's all. Voices that fit together. Chemistry, molecules. They could've been Siamese twins sharing a common nose, a couple of sisters with three eyes, the Everly Humpbacks. Gimme early Elvis, Carl Perkins, gimme Chuck Berry, outta that period. I listen to jazz now, little brother, me and Jenny."

The way he said that, you'd think Jenny was his wife. Jennie Sweetie. Lyle and her on the loveseat, a jazz combo on the CD player, Chardonnay in crystal on the teak end tables. *Ooo lah lah.*

Guess again. Jenny was his cat. I'm pretty sure Jenny's a male, too, but Lyle wouldn't say. Wouldn't admit that the name Jenny's from the Everly Brothers song, either.

You see what I mean?

e⌒

And don't tell me about the Everly Brothers' reunion. It proved nothing.

After ten long years apart, love conquers all. Sure, and I'm Charlemagne.

As If No Time Had Passed!

Pure claptrap. Staged, I tell you. Staged every step of the way. Remember to smile for the nice people. They looked at each other and there was Zip. Not a thing. The years had not been kind. This I saw with my own eyes. *The movie wasn't so hot.* I'm telling you the reunion was nothing but cold hard cash. I saw both concerts at the Albert Hall. Believe in that reunion? *Wake up, little Susie.*

e⌒

After we didn't go to the Knott's Berry Farm concert in '73, there was a hiatus between calls. A seven-year hiatus.

Actually, I called him one more time. It was a week before I came to California, just to see if Lyle wanted to get together for dinner while I was there. Skip the concert if he wanted, I'd still be in the neighborhood.

"Next week? I'm in, let's see, La Paz Monday and Tuesday, Sao Paulo and Rio Wednesday–Thursday, fly to Mazatlan Friday for a little R&R. No can do, I guess. Sorry little brother."

I didn't say, "You knew I was coming." *It happens every time.* Instead, I said, "Maybe next time."

Then after seven years, Lyle heard I had health problems. Health problems? Only two plugged arteries, nothing to worry about. I was thirty-three at the time.

He heard this from our cousin Davey, who lived in Beverly Hills not far from Lyle. But then, what was far from Lyle?

Davey always got me rock 'n' roll memorabilia, which wasn't difficult where he lived, but I appreciated it. He found some early Beach Boys posters, a Ricky Nelson guitar pick allegedly used when he recorded "Believe What You Say." Who can be sure? He got me the top hat they put on a basset hound the time Elvis sang "Hound Dog" on Steve Allen's show and wasn't allowed to wiggle his hips. Good stuff, but the only Everly Brothers article Davey ever snagged for me was a 1958 *Billboard* ad saying "Everlys Record in New York." Their producer had a fit over this ad because she didn't want anybody to think Don and Phil would go uptown.

"A great find. Thanks a lot, cuz."

I'm sure Lyle would've done the same thing for me if he'd come across it first.

Memorabilia was how Davey and I stayed in touch. Our staying in touch was how he knew about my health problems.

How come he and Lyle stayed in touch I do not know. Maybe because they were big time globetrotters, both ritzy guys, self-made, right out of high school and into the world. Davey's in films. I see his name in the credits from time to time, for technical stuff.

He doesn't seem to mind talking to a historian once in a while. A medievalist, no less, who also happens to like fifties music. What can I say? I also like "Sir Gawain and the Green Knight."

Seven years, then I picked up the phone and it was Lyle. Not beating around the bush, he said, "Hi little brother, tell me exactly what the doctor said."

I laughed. Not for the reason Lyle thought, which was because I was disconcerted by his approach. That was what wanted, to get me flustered.

No, I laughed because this Everly Brothers line zinged into my head: *I feel a brand-new heartache coming on,* and I almost said it. Then I had a flash of Lyle's face, with his eyes crossing and his tongue trying to reach his nose. Or anyway, Lyle's face from 1960 or so, the face he'd use when he was trying to show contempt.

"The doctor says rampant cholesterol. Says if I cut it in half, it'd still be in the danger zone. Says even at my age, it makes me a high risk for a heart attack and it's a good thing I don't smoke, I exercise, and my diet's low in cholesterol. Or I'd be dead already. He thinks two valves are almost out of business already."

"Heredity?"

Guess by now you know that I'm devoted to you.

"Yes."

"Should I be worried?"

"No, I'm taking medication. I'll be okay. The doctor says they might not have to operate."

"I meant about me, little brother. We do have the same parents. Plus I do smoke, I don't exercise, and I eat lots and lots of nasty fats. So why am I still alive and plucky at forty-one, while you're plugging up at thirty-three?"

I should have known.

"Apparently we don't have the same genes. You'll live to be a hundred."

"Same parents, different genes? That's how I always saw it, myself."

ℰ

The original Everly Brothers team was composed of the father, Ike, and his two brothers up in Chicago. Then over in Iowa, the mother asked if the boys wanted to sing on the radio too and bam: You've got the Everly Family on KMA before school.

What a nice piece of history. They probably got straight A's, milked the cows, and delivered the afternoon papers too. America!

How about this one: It was 1960 and the boys had two Number One Hits already. They'd cut eight records, done tours, the whole shebang. Phil was back living with the parents when Don called and said come over to my house, help me finish this song I'm writing.

Bam: Two days later they recorded "Cathy's Clown," their all-time best seller. *I die each time I hear this sound.*

This happened. Like their voices, these guys bobbed right along, they glistened. And they owed it all to ma and pa. Just like me and Lyle. *You don't realize what you do to me.*

Only our home life was a little different than the Everlys'. I'm not saying it's our parents' fault that Lyle and I didn't have a string of hits. I'm not even sure it's fair to say we owe what we are, or how we are, to them.

But home was where we learned how to treat each other. Of that I'm sure. Which is why, when I watched Phil Everly stomp off stage that night at Knott's Berry Farm, I thought, *oh no, I don't need to see this.*

℮

Our father had his one massive coronary in 1961. That was all it took.

As a youth, he didn't quit Kentucky coal mines like Ike Everly. Nor did he move to Chicago with his brothers and begin singing for a living, thereby opening the future for his sons.

Our father also didn't quit his Brooklyn hardware store to sing with his brothers in Manhattan. No quitting, no singing. Quitting would have been sensational, but it was just as well since all he had were sisters and none sang worth a damn, which they proved at every family get-together in the fifties.

In fact, our father did not quit his Brooklyn hardware store to play with me or Lyle, or to attend ball games with us or school plays, or to visit us in summer camp. However, he did stop up to see Lyle in the hospital the time he had surgery on his eye. I'll give him that.

It probably would have been better for me and Lyle if our father didn't hit us at the dinner table. The backhand thwack, then green peas or half-chewed meat all over the table.

The way it worked, Mom would report our daily doings between her trips to the kitchen to clear dirty dishes and bring on the next course. Dad would eat less and less of each course until she'd stop—with a full plate of flank steak and green peas in her hand—and say, "Marv, don't you like the flank steak anymore?"

Right about there was where he'd hit us.

I've got a dining room table in my house now that's so long you could play shuffleboard on it. Hitting at the table is out.

Mom showed us a nifty way to deal with family problems, as represented by Dad. She kept clear of him.

She stayed up all night, turning in at about 3:30 a.m. when he was just waking up. Then she woke up shortly after noon and was really rolling when he'd come home at 7:00 p.m. So she was at her best right when he was fading.

They had about ninety minutes to get through together every day and most of that was dinner, when she was bustling from the kitchen to the dining room. Me and Lyle took the brunt of that time. Then he'd retire and she'd write letters. *Love hurts.*

&

I don't keep track, but this must be the year for my septennial phone call from Lyle. We both still appear to be alive.

He starts right in, as if we'd last spoken on Thursday.

"What's it like, little brother?"

I know what he's talking about. After all, it is on my mind, since I'm in the hospital and awfully sore. Open heart at forty. Almost unheard of, but those weren't muscle spasms in my chest. The tests confirmed that.

"It's not bad, Lyle. Sort of like running into a circular saw."

"Cheer up. Didn't you get my gift?"

The last time Lyle gave me a gift was in 1959. It was a small record player with a thick spindle for playing 45s. Great gift. But he'd never let me borrow his records, so all I could play on it were a couple of Dion & the Belmonts songs that Lyle got tired of and gave to me.

His new gift arrived yesterday. It's a tape player, small enough to fit on the bed beside me, with earphones and great sound. Inside was *The Everly Brothers 24 Original Classics.*

I start light exercise this week. They say there's very little I won't be able to do after the convalescence ends. It's all in the head, and my heart's fine now.

Everybody gets depressed after bypass surgery, so the fact that I need a little help right now isn't something to worry about. The thing is to get centered, or something like that. Cemented? Wintered?

I'm supposed to decide to live a long, active life. I'm supposed to realize that I can be well. And then, bam: I will be well.

Makes sense to me. Doesn't it make sense to you?

Imagine that, Lyle sending me an Everly Brothers tape. *Last night I cried myself to sleep.*

Karaoke Night at the Trail's End

Jake Innis liked coming to The Trail's End for their burgers, but that alone wouldn't have been enough to justify the hour's drive. He liked its ambience—men wearing string ties and cowboy boots with collapsed heels, women dancing in skin-tight jeans and white-ruffled vee-neck blouses—but that wasn't what brought him all the way to the little town of Concord either. Halfway to the coast, snug in the foothills of the Sunset Mountains, Concord had just over a thousand residents and no bank, no pharmacy, no gas station, not even a barber shop. It did have The Trail's End, though, and Karaoke Night every Thursday, which fell smack in the middle of Jake's weekend. But even that was not what brought him to Concord, though he hadn't missed a Karaoke Night in six months, and the regulars sure hoped it was why the little guy in baggy khakis and striped rugby shirts kept showing up.

He came because of the concentrations. For over a year, Jake had been searching for a place where the pressure felt balanced, where he could breathe right. First he had tried downtown bars, then started going to suburban hangouts, moving in a widening circle until he had driven clear through the four metropolitan area counties and found his way to Concord. He walked into The Trail's End one April night and remembered trout from his childhood summers, the ones his father would throw back into the lake. They'd just float for a few seconds as though stunned to be back in their element, shiver like they were shaking off the memory of air, then flash deep and zoom out of sight. He imagined they had suddenly felt through their entire bodies an absolute sense of rightness, of arrival, *here it is!* That was what Jake felt in the doorway of The Trail's End that first time. Perhaps, he thought later, it was just that he'd at last come far enough west-southwest to escape the feeling of proximity to his office, of availability by accident if someone saw him and wanted to talk about a case, a call, a death.

Being a 9-1-1 operator was supposed to have been a temporary situation. It was something to do between jobs while he picked up a few more credits toward his degree in counseling. But now he was the senior member of the staff. He'd heard murders and suicides, berserk babysitters, children in the grip of bogeymen, rapes and robberies and fires and car wrecks and asthma attacks, lonely old people in the middle of the night, just about everything the system could throw at him. If he saved another five or six thousand bucks, he could finally quit and go back to school full time, get the degree in a couple of years and start doing what he really wanted to do. Help people.

The way Jake saw it, Karaoke Night was like a seminar in psychology anyway. He used to take notes, till the regulars made it clear from their expressions that perhaps he ought to wait till he got home to write anything down. Which he did for a while too, but not for the last couple months. Now he was content just to watch and listen. Might keep track of something like the ratio of country to rock, or maintain an ongoing ranking of performances for the evening, just to stay alert to the nuances, but nothing more professional than that.

Back in his apartment, Jake had been working on his rendition of "I Can't Stop Loving You." It wasn't ready yet. Soon, maybe. He had worked for five solid weeks on "At the Hop," the old Danny & the Juniors hit from the winter of 1958, something his father used to sing when he got drunk enough. The plan had been to get the song down perfectly, then audition it at some Karaoke joint in the city, probably that Chinese restaurant around the corner from his apartment, the Szechuan Cove. They had Karaoke Night on Wednesdays, which might work, though Jake would be a little tired. It was like taking a Broadway show out to Boston for a tryout. Afterwards, he'd smooth the song's rough spots in his apartment before its premiere at The Trail's End. But at the last minute he had decided to scrap both the plan and the song. "At the Hop" was too damned fast anyway, you could hardly get the words out even if you knew them by heart, and what if the words on the screen didn't keep pace with the music? Because if they did, they'd have to be scrolling along so damned quick he wouldn't be able to read them anyway. A ballad, that was the answer. He'd be ready next week. The week after, tops.

Tonight there was quite a crowd though, maybe twenty people more than usual, which made it tempting for Jake to consider unleashing "I Can't Stop Loving You," despite the risk. He'd been thinking about it for the last hour. Most of the singers so far had been doing safe old stuff, lots of Elvis tunes, which are always a cinch, or "Wooly Bully" and "La Bamba," mush like "Time After Time." Nothing that took much talent. One woman did a passable

"Chain of Fools," but it was a slow night. When he finally picked up the mike, Jake planned to knock them out. They were certainly set up for him tonight.

After a break, this tall, slender woman in a dark green dress came up to the stage. She had enormous hands and full lips, but everything about her seemed small. Her black hair stood straight up on top, like dune grass, and was cut so short on the sides that her scalp showed through. She looked decimated, as though she hadn't eaten in weeks, but her dress was elegant and her hairdo had cost sincere dollars. Something else about her, something other than her startling appearance, grabbed Jake's attention. She was nervous, but not the way most people got nervous. It seemed like she was shrinking before his eyes as the place quieted slightly and the host tested his equipment.

Jake suddenly felt he understood what was happening. Please, God, let her be able to carry a tune. Because she was obviously falling apart already and the song hadn't even begun. He knew the look: She was about to plunge over the parapet, jump on board the speeding express, shoot the works. He didn't know if he was prepared to see it happen.

Lenny Eaves, whose golden-wigged wife Jolene ran The Trail's End and sat at the register conditioning her cuticles, announced that the woman's name was Gail. He staggered back as though being buffeted by a gale wind and smiled, dentures blazing in the spotlights.

"So let's hear it for a crazy little lady named Gail!"

Few people bothered to clap. Jake guessed the noise was equivalent to wax-paper wrappings from around two Trail's End Burgers being crumpled simultaneously. So he upped the ante by smacking the edge of the bar. Then a man sitting right in front of the stage got up, staggering toward the bathroom, and scattered laughter drowned out the meager applause.

Great, just what she needs, a laugh-track. Gail was standing sideways to the audience, knees bent, shoulders hunched, hands wrapped tightly around the microphone. She held it clutched against her chest like a charm and looked thoroughly ashamed of herself. Her eyes seemed transfixed to the screen where the words to her song would appear, but she didn't move or blink.

Jake couldn't watch. He signaled to the bartender for another beer, then gulped the last warm dregs of his old one. He folded up his napkin and empty pack of nuts, and stuffed them inside the mug.

Crazy, Gail moaned.

She dragged out the two syllables and bit her lower lip. The music continued but Gail just stood there, eyes now closed, nodding as though agreeing with her initial assessment. Jake held his breath. Gail took a deep breath of her own, as though going after the air Jake wasn't using, and added, *I'm crazy for wanting to hold you.*

What? Wait! Cut! Jake looked around to see if anyone else had noticed her mistake. So far, so good, no one was paying attention. He lifted his mug to his lips but couldn't sip.

Gail rolled her head as though loosening up her neck, eyes still shut, and sang, *I'm crazy, crazy for seeing this through.*

Read the words, Gail! Jake had never seen the woman before, but he found himself excruciatingly embarrassed for her and the song was only three lines old. Oh please, honey, open your eyes. He looked closely at her, willing her to snap out of it, but even though Gail was standing in the spotlight she seemed completely hidden. He tried to focus on her eyes. Maybe she's Japanese, maybe this is how they do Karaoke over there. The Japanese dreamed up the idea in the first place, perhaps they prefer making up their own words to the songs and that's how it's supposed to work. But Jake knew she was no more Asian than he was, and he'd heard a number of Japanese Karaoke singers in town who did get the lyrics right, even if it was clear they had no idea what the words meant. Jake opened his own eyes as widely as he could, hoping to pry hers open by telepathy.

You do, she sang, and then stopped again. Jake was not going to make it. He shifted on the stool, unable to look away as she plunged ahead: *Not one thing that I ever wanted.*

It was amazing. The sense of the song was right and so were the rhymes, but hardly any of the words. Did she know what she was doing? Didn't she practice? Patsy Cline, for God's sake, summer of '61. It's not exactly Keats. Willie Nelson wrote the thing, darlin', let's sing it right. Although Jake was getting the feeling these words were no mistake either.

He wished everyone would shut up so he could concentrate on her more clearly. She needed help and it seemed as though he might be the only one around who could give it to her. Jake was now off his stool, resting his back on the bar, and his hands were crossed over his chest almost like Gail's. Whiskey, that's what he needed, forget beer.

And yet somehow, you held me there closer to you.

Jake suddenly remembered a call he'd had at work about eight months ago. This was another thing that bothered him about his job, the way old calls would appear across his mind like e-mail, zipping right onto the screen while he was busy doing something else. They broke in in a way that couldn't be ignored. So now he found himself hearing that guy from back in February or March quite plainly, his deep raspy voice uttering neat little sentences of pure gibberish. The tone was calm and rational. Each phrase was perfectly constructed to sound like normally inflected English, but the words were unintelligible, the language of sheer madness. *Valkesch, cumph jeripono bala arnguise. Mairlinz. Mairlinz.* The guy had gone on like that for forty seconds before hanging up. He had placed the call from a phone booth near the city's Civic Auditorium and vanished by the time a patrol car arrived. Jake had played the tape back half a dozen times, trying to unscramble the words, saying them backwards, working with a couple of the other operators to break the code. Normally, 9-1-1 operators reported prank calls and forgot about them, but Jake couldn't get rid of the feeling that this one was directed right at him and that there was a message in them if he could only discover it. He even placed calls to the phone booth three different nights at the same time the original call had been made, but no one ever answered. Within a few weeks, he realized how absurd the idea was and tried to let it go. But the call still left him restless and worried. No one else got one like it. Edna, who sat at the console next to Jake's, suggested that the call had come from an alien. Over and over, she said it was the only possible explanation, and Jake couldn't tell if she was teasing him or not. He dreamed that he was in church and suddenly seized by a fit, falling to the floor, writhing there while he babbled in tongues, surrounded by a congregation of strangers taking notes on his testifying. He dreamed that a Brahma bull came leaping and roaring into his bedroom through the cat's door, then turned to attack him, snorting the words *Mairlinz! Mairlinz!* The whole experience left Jake feeling edgy, especially at night after work. It wasn't long before he began searching for a suitable Karaoke place. Gail's voice came back higher and somewhat wilder after the brief musical bridge. She seemed to be reaching out and lifting Jake's chin with the finger of her voice so that he had no choice but to look at her. But she kept her eyes clamped tight.

Sorry. How can I stop feeling sorry. She really had a lovely voice, full of longing, clear as mountain wind.

It took all Jake's self-control to keep himself from calling out to her. What do you have to feel sorry about? He's just using you, you said so yourself.

This would never do. He turned his back to the stage and started folding his fresh napkin into smaller and smaller halves. Jake had read that one of the problems counselors face is over-identifying with their clients. There were courses in that, he knew, but Jake hadn't taken one. Still, he should be able to handle things better. He unfolded his napkin. He took a few sips of beer, then put the mug down with a thump, watching as a drop splashed onto his napkin and seeped through its layers.

He turned to the stage again, having missed most of her chorus. *I'm sorry I found you, and sorry I lost you, and I'm sorry for wanting you.*

She was finished, thank God. To faint applause, Gail handed the microphone to Lenny Eaves and left the stage, heading directly to the bathroom. Didn't these people know what they'd just heard? Forget the miracle of the lyrics, Gail's chesty, soulful, accurate voice alone was enough to warrant a major ovation. For most singers here, melody was an obstacle to be dodged. Jake clapped hard for her. It had no effect on the rest of the crowd, however, because Lenny began talking about the next singer, a trucker named Mobley Barnes, who of course was going to perform "The House of the Rising Sun," which he'd sung every Thursday now since Jake first showed up.

Jake hadn't gotten a good look at Gail's face, but he could tell she wasn't smiling as she left the stage. In fact, she seemed flushed and close to tears, but that could just be a trick of his angle of view or of the lights. He looked around for a table with a vacant chair and a woman's coat hung over the back, or for a half-finished glass of chablis. There, over by the dart board and video games, where the waitresses stacked dirty dishes. An empty table with a full, frosty mug of beer waiting on the side that faced the stage and, draped across the rest of the table as though to discourage anyone from sitting there, a beat-up black leather bomber's-jacket. He thought it had to be Gail's.

He took his beer, walked over to the table and sat down, elbowing the jacket to one side. In all the time he'd been coming to The Trail's End, Jake had never tried to pick up a woman, never engaged anyone in more than a casual conversation about the weather or the playoffs or the virtues of smoked almonds. At most, he'd exchanged glances when a singer was particularly awful or, rarely, wonderful. Yet here he was, sitting at Gail's table uninvited, waiting for her to get back from the bathroom, without the slightest inkling of what he intended to say to her. Part of him wanted to encourage her to keep telling the story, let it all out. He was there for her. Part of him wanted to tell her his own story, though he didn't exactly know what that story might be. Alas, part of him wanted to correct her lyrics, but he was confident he could keep that part under control.

Mobley Barnes was deep into his lament about a sad New Orleans childhood and everybody in the place seemed spellbound. Jake shook his head. The Animals, late summer of '64. Suddenly, Gail was standing behind him as though she'd simply materialized from inside one of the video games. She looked down at Jake as though trying to remember if she knew him, and did not speak. Then she walked past him and sat at a table with two other women, each of whom immediately scooted her chair closer to Gail's and flung an arm around her shoulders, their hands coming to rest on one another's forearms. They leaned close, whispering to her simultaneously, kissing her cheeks, and then all three women sat back to squelch their laughter with hands raised to their mouths.

As usual, Mobley Barnes's voice sailed completely out of its range and disappeared as he neared his finale. Jake hustled back to the bar, glad to have escaped before the owner of that bomber-jacket noticed him. Just what he needed, put the make on some guy who came in here on a Harley. Maybe it was Mobley Barnes's table.

Jake was also glad to see that Gail wasn't rushing to leave. He tried to figure out what her look had meant, a dreamy gaze of perhaps partial recognition, but he couldn't be sure that she had even registered his presence. What was he thinking, stationing himself at a table like that waiting to take her by surprise? If it had gone as he'd planned it, she'd probably have shrieked *Mairlinz! Mairlinz!* and fled out the front door.

Of course surprise isn't good. Jake knew that well enough from his experience at work. Every year he handled half a dozen accidental domestic shootings, people appearing unexpectedly in their own bedroom doorways. Keep your wits about you, Jake Innis. So you don't just occupy her territory uninvited. What, then?

Okay, Mr. Counselor, you caught a break. Regroup. Go figure out what you're after while you finish your beer. You want to meet this woman, is that it? You have something to say to her? Great, here comes another cowboy singing "Proud Mary," which rules out coherent thought. Jake drained his beer.

He took out a pen, spread his napkin on the bar like a sheet of stationery, and began doodling. Spirals leading to circles within cross-hatched cubes. It didn't take a degree in quantum physics: She's the first kindred spirit you've found since you starting hanging out in Karaoke bars, you knew it as soon as she went off the trail. Pouring her heart out in song. Only she went one better. Not only got up there and sang, which anybody can do, witness Mobley Barnes or this guy with his big wheel rolling, even you someday, Innis. But Gail told her own story, which takes real character. That is, of course, unless she simply screwed up the lyrics. Or was loony, which Jake didn't believe. He looked over to her table and saw that she was alone now. Her friends must have left, must have stayed just long enough to hear Gail sing and then headed back to the city. But without her. Jake wondered if that meant she was planning an encore. Make up her own words to "Louie Louie," nobody would know the difference.

He did need to talk to her. Jake saw that clearly. It was the same feeling he had those three nights when he called the phone booth near the Civic Auditorium. But he wasn't comfortable with the idea of marching over there again, in case she'd really noticed him that first time. Besides, he knew he couldn't mention liking her song without also mentioning what she did with the lyrics, and he thought that would be a mistake.

Only one thing to do. "Proud Mary" was over, so was Lenny

Eaves's banter while he waited for the next singer, and it looked like they were about to take a break because there were no volunteers. Gail must be resting her voice. Jake got up and walked toward the stage. So what if he didn't have all the flaws worked out with his song, sometimes a man just has to take a chance.

"Here we go," said Lenny. "One more singer before we get to freshen up. Tell you what folks, here at The Trail's End we been wondering for months if this young man was ever going to come up and sing for us. Don't even know his name."

He stuck the microphone in Jake's face and smiled. Jake said, "I Can't Stop Loving You."

"No wonder he didn't tell us his name before!"

There were a few titters. Jake was afraid to turn around now because he knew he'd blushed vermilion. He'd just have to hope Gail was still there, and not among the laughers.

"Sorry. I'm Jake Innis."

"All right, let's hear it for Jake the Rake." There was some applause and Jake slowly turned around, but couldn't see much from within the lights. Lenny, still speaking into the microphone, said "Now I'm sorry to tell you this, Jake, but we don't have 'I Can't Stop Loving You' on our playlist. Got something else for us?"

Oh God, no! Jake took a quick look at the list that Lenny thrust into his hand. He was barely able to concentrate. Of course, right near the top was "At the Hop," but that was out of the question. He returned the list to Lenny and took two steps back, ready to leave the stage. Then, astonished at what he was doing, he strode forward again, took the microphone and said, "Eleanor Rigby."

"Done," said Lenny.

Jake didn't hear what else Lenny said because he was trying to

137

figure out what he was going to do. He couldn't bring himself to turn and face front. Then almost before he knew what was happening, the pulsating opening notes of the song began to repeat themselves. He thought, but didn't sing, *Ah, look at all the lonely people.* He thought, summer of '66, flip side of "Yellow Submarine." Then he lifted the microphone to his mouth.

Girl in a green dress, he sang, looking toward the screen where words were scrolling, then looking away. *Makes up the words to a song as she stands on the stage.*

He tried to find the table where he knew Gail had been sitting, but still couldn't see well. He moved to his left, out of the spotlight, and tried to pick her out.

Isn't afraid. There, the right table, but empty. Out of the corner of his eye he saw someone moving toward the door. *Tells me a story, based on her life that is filling her soul up with pain.* She went out without looking back. Had she heard him? Was she offended? He hoped not, and he realized it didn't matter that she was gone. Jake took a quick breath and moved back into the light.

Don't be ashamed. He shifted the microphone, closed his eyes and belted out the lines: *All the sorry couples, they do not get along. All the sorry couples, where have they all gone wrong?*

III

The Wings of the Wind

He came swiftly upon the wings
of the wind.

He made darkness his covering
around him.

—Psalm 18

My son Isaac, adopted at twelve weeks of age, turned twenty on September fifteenth. That day, he measured seven feet five and three-quarter inches tall. When he was home last summer, I stood beside him posing for a photograph and my head came up to about his pancreas.

Isaac outgrew Loretta when he was eight and me when he was ten. But until he was sixteen or so, he loved to walk between us holding hands, towering over us like a spike on a graph. He would giggle at our reflections in shop windows and at the looks on the faces of passers-by. Isaac weighs exactly what my wife and I do combined, two hundred ninety pounds. And as you can see, I'm accustomed to using precise numbers when I speak of my son.

Loretta and I got him from an orphanage in The People's Republic of Romania at the zenith of Ceausescu's power. All we knew was that he'd been born near Sibiu, a small industrial city north of the Transylvania Alps, his mother had been a textile worker, and he had such raging impetigo around his nose and mouth when we first saw him that it looked as though someone had drawn on a bright red clown's face.

We named him Isaac after my father, but the name would have had a nice resonance for us anyway. According to Genesis, the biblical Isaac was born when his parents were quite old and thought themselves well beyond child-bearing age. Same as us. He was also the fulfillment of a promise, which felt right in our case as well, a kind of entitlement due to a couple who loved as deeply as we did. Then what does God do after giving Sarah and Abraham their son? Right, order the boy slaughtered. No wonder Loretta and I were overprotective, despite our Isaac's size.

He was virtually silent during the entire plane trip from Bucharest to New York. He slept for long periods, waking with a soft whimper wanting to be fed, then sitting in his carrier with his eyes wide open, hands moving vaguely in front of his face as though warding off something strange and unpleasant. His smiles seemed wholly inward, prompted less by anything he saw than by forces going on inside his body.

Probably you've heard of him. Isaac Berg, the great basketball star. Most people call him Ike and the press dubbed him The Ikeberg, a huge mass afloat in the middle of the lane. They said he might be the best collegiate center since either Wilt Chamberlain or Kareem Abdul-Jabbar or Bill Walton or Shaquille O'Neal—depending on your era—and maybe the best big man ever. In his freshman year at the University of Oregon, Isaac averaged twenty-six points, fourteen rebounds and six blocked shots a game, leading the Ducks to the NCAA Final Four where absolutely no one had expected them to be and where they'd never been before. People in and around the game thought he'd leave school then and make himself eligible for the pro draft, but he stayed on and had an even better sophomore year. In a press conference last spring, to stop all the speculation, he announced that he was staying in school for his final two years. He wanted to get his degree, help the team to its third straight Final Four appearance, and play in the Olympics as a true amateur before basketball became a job for him.

I hope you got to see my Isaac during that press conference. Except for his size, everything about him said *Gentle Scholar,* said *Books,* said *Soulful.* For the first time, his nickname seemed to make sense, to reflect the truth that so much of Isaac was hidden below the surface regardless of how much there was above it. After every question, he looked down as though to collect his thoughts, smiling shyly, humble, unwilling to seem the smart-ass like so many other young athletes. It was the proudest moment for me, prouder than all his on-court honors, prouder than the night he scored sixty-seven points and grabbed twenty-eight rebounds against UCLA.

The name Isaac Berg, I would be the first to admit, fits a little strangely on him now. We had him circumcised when he was an infant, brought him up within the Reform movement as a moderately observant Jew, and kept telling him that he, of all people, was truly one of the *Chosen.* Of course, he looks about as Jewish as Vlad the Impaler, but who knew that when he was six years old? He was a dark infant, had huge hands and feet, a mop of curly black hair and deep-set eyes that followed me everywhere I moved, and while I didn't think he was necessarily of Jewish parentage, I didn't imagine he would look quite so gentile either. His features became enormous, everything growing at an accelerated pace, and, with his *basso profundo* voice thrown in, my son could be quite terrifying to encounter. Which is so ironic, since I believe it worries him to box opponents out for a rebound lest he accidentally crush someone.

At his Bar Mitzvah, Isaac stood six foot five and towered above the rabbi. Most thirteen-year-olds have to stand on a stool to see over the podium when they read their Bar Mitzvah portions to the congregation. Isaac, clean-shaven but heavily shadowed with stubble by 10:00 a.m., had to stoop so that Rabbi Herschorn didn't hurt himself looking up to bless the Bar Mitzvah boy. As Isaac carried the Torah in a slow march through the congregation, some of the little old men reaching up to touch the scroll with the hems of their prayer shawls suddenly backed away as though seeing a Cossack on horseback. But he was oblivious, blissful at being a newly consecrated member of the tribe, his face aglow as he passed into light that poured through the stained glass window at the rear of the sanctuary. That night, at home after his party, Isaac couldn't stop talking about feeling hugged by God. Those were his exact words. He'd been embraced in that light, taken over, and felt himself to be loved and protected forever. It was a feeling I have never had myself, even at his age, and I remember hoping that whatever caused him to lose it wouldn't be too great for him to bear.

Like so many extremely tall young people, Isaac had his social difficulties, especially as an adolescent. He didn't join clubs, didn't have any close male friends, didn't date much. The first time, near the end of his sophomore year, he asked me to drive him and the young girl, a foreign exchange student from Paris named Laura Quost, to the downtown cinema where a French film was showing. I dropped them off, went by myself to another film in a theater across the river, then picked them up four hours later at the Metro on Broadway, where they'd gone for snacks and sparkling water. Isaac's relief when he saw me walk through the restaurant's doors was so palpable that I felt like crying for him.

He knew he was strange-looking and, I think, secretly agreed when kids called him Frankenstein, called him Moonman, Geek or Bronto. But that all changed halfway through his junior year in high school, when Isaac's talent as a basketball player asserted itself and he became a hero over the course of one frigid Portland winter.

I'll never forgot the silence that fell over the gym the first time Isaac's rage was expressed on the court. The silence only lasted for two seconds, a kind of collective stoppage of breath, before turning into something like joy as the fans erupted in whistles and wild cheers. But it was those two seconds I'll never forget. Isaac had been taunted by the opposing fans and, worse, by players on the other team, throughout the first half of the season's opening game. He'd refused even to consider joining the team during his first two years in school, refused to be seen with a basketball anywhere except on the driveway beside our house, and as the game progressed he had played mildly, passing the ball off whenever he got it, sticking up his arms but not moving aggressively to block any shots, reaching for rebounds but not boxing-out or jumping. It seemed as though he was afraid to stumble and look awkward, though I knew it had more to do with his fear of causing harm.

As the third quarter was drawing to a close, I saw his eyes narrow and his nostrils flare and I felt that something had snapped in Isaac. After all those years of being razzed, of trying to act small, denying his essential isolation, he'd finally grasped some essential truth about his situation and reached an instantaneous decision. He moved into position at the top of the key and raised his arms, calling for the ball. The point guard, as shocked as I was to see Isaac asserting his will, bounced the pass to him. Isaac planted his feet, spun to his left and took one incredibly long step toward the basket. With the ball securely stuck in his right palm, he threw down a slam dunk in one great windmilling motion. The ball tore through the net and bounced back up off the floor so high that time seemed to stand still as everyone watched it reach its apogee before reacting to what they had seen. Isaac had dunked from the foul line, moving through the air with such power, authority and grace that he looked like a seasoned professional. Or a prehistoric bird riding a zephyr. Back on the ground, he stood there glaring into the middle distance while the gym filled with noise. Then his eyes changed again, found me where I sat at midcourt as he trotted back on defense, and the expression on my son's face was a terrifying mix of triumph and grief.

Believe me, there was never a spoken plan. However, Loretta and I understood that Isaac intended to buy us a new home on Lake Oswego as soon as he signed his first professional contract. He thought we might also like matching leather recliners for the new living room, a big-screen television on which to watch his games, a dark green Lexus, a summer trip to Israel after the basketball season. Where he came up with Israel, I don't know. My fantasy has always been a month on the beach in Rio.

This idea of Isaac's was something we knew from hints and suggestions he would drop into conversations. We'd be sitting in the living room after dinner, all three of us immersed in our books, and Isaac would suddenly wonder if it'd be nice to listen to some Mozart right about now, maybe that Piano Concerto in C Major that we all went to hear last year in downtown Portland. Be nice to savor the clear sound one of those new CD players is capable of. Then furniture and electronics catalogues started to arrive for us in the mail after his freshman season at Oregon. We were suddenly on the mailing lists for travel agencies and fancy automobile dealerships. Taking care of us in this way was probably the only thing that made Isaac hesitate to turn down the professional inducements and stay in school till he graduated. I'm glad he did.

These dreams on our behalf were pure American dreams. They certainly weren't Romanian ones. So equating personal success with waterfront homes or luxury cars isn't in our genes after all! Tay-Sachs disease is in our genes, a hundred times more than in anybody else's, but not the need for a big-screen television. Excuse me. I've been a bit emotional lately.

Although Isaac's dreams for us were contagious as airborne viruses, and we couldn't help talking from time to time about when we would be living on the lake, I'd have been happy—and I'm confident Loretta would have been happy, too—just to see Isaac at ease in this world we had brought him to, see him pleased with his achievements in it and smiling as he looked it in its eye. Of course, I'd also like to have a view of water. But so would my

147

friend Henry Ah Sing, who owns a restaurant in Old Town and is far more likely to get such a view than I am.

Because three months, one week and two days ago, on a typically dark, windy December night in eastern Washington, I watched Isaac follow his own missed sky-hook shot with a brilliant rebound and slam dunk over the seven-foot Nigerian center who plays for Washington State, turn to head back downcourt, come to a complete stop while everyone ran by him, raise his arms a few inches toward his breastbone, and crumple to the court as though he'd been shot. He hit the wood floor so hard that I could hear the sound of it over the wildly beating drum that Cougar fans were using to whip themselves into a frenzy as they urged their team on. I swear I could feel it through my toes.

The team doctor rushed onto the court. He threw himself onto his knees and skidded to a stop beside Isaac, jerking open a bag as he reached toward my son's chest. Almost instantly, they were surrounded by members of the team, all of them too large to see past.

The image that stayed before my eyes was of Isaac's utter stillness there. He lay sprawled across the top of the key, his face down and twisted slightly to the left in a position just like the one he always slept in as an infant. My first thought, odd and unbeckoned, was that I was glad Loretta's arthritis was acting up so that she'd decided against coming to Pullman with me.

I got up to run onto the court, but was restrained by some people sitting nearby. Their collective grip on my arms and shoulders—part embrace, part shackles—felt as though it were cutting off my air supply. I shook myself free and ran onto the court. The videotapes played over and over again on the news, especially the

one on ESPN, shows my mouth opening and closing as though I
were screaming, but nothing was coming out. To me, it looked like
I was trying to breathe for Isaac.

Technically, he was already dead when he hit the floor. But
I didn't need to be told that. As I watched him fall, I swear I
glimpsed a faint spray like the sweat that comes off a boxer's face
when you see a slow-motion film of him taking an uppercut to
the jaw. I understood that this was the spirit rising out of Isaac,
a soft blue incandescence, it seemed to me, the actual formation
of an aura around his collapsing form. When I knelt beside him,
Isaac's gigantic body seemed vacated and when I touched the cen-
ter of his limp palm—his most ticklish spot—there was nothing.

Miraculously, it turned out that Marius DePino, the west
coast's premier heart surgeon, was in the crowd. This was certainly
the first and most profound of our blessings that night.

Dr. DePino had come from Seattle to tour the campus with
his youngest son, who wanted to become a veterinarian. When
they'd heard that Oregon would be playing at Washington State,
they stayed to see the great Isaac Berg in person. Dr. DePino
quickly made his way down from the stands and trotted onto the
court, working through the circle around Isaac's form until he was
beside my son. His hand brushed my shoulder gently, asking me
to step aside.

Marius DePino brought my son back and kept him here,
turning the visitors' locker room into an emergency room (while
getting me to scribble a waiver of liability on the back of a
Cougars-Ducks souvenir program) and working on my son's heart
before my eyes. The inventor of the DePino Procedure for cor-
recting mitral valve prolapse and of the DePino Technique for

grafting veins in bypass surgeries, the author of two cardiology textbooks and a popular novel about the mystical bond between a heart transplant recipient and his donor's daughter, the man was both brilliant and bold. I don't remember anything after seeing DePino's hands begin moving toward Isaac's chest. The team doctor got to work on me while DePino worked on my son.

There was more surgery later, after he was stable, to correct Isaac's hypertrophic cardiomyopathy, a thickening of the inner wall of his heart's pumping chamber. Usually, this disease can only be discovered after its young victim has died a sudden death. This is why I'm supposed to regard Isaac as lucky. They put a small electronic defibrillator behind his stomach muscles to shock his heart back into rhythm whenever it goes haywire on him.

Isaac always wondered how to get closer to God. To me now, it feels like he is—the Lord's hand present in tiny heartshocks emanating from Isaac's belly. But what it feels like to me isn't what it feels like to my son.

You see film clips on the news all the time. These very tall young men in the greatest physical condition imaginable, these invincible kids on the brink of vast fortunes, suddenly collapse on the court. One minute, they slam dunk and make the whole backboard shake or they swat a shot into the fourth row, and the next minute, they're dead. Hank Gathers of Loyola Marymount, dead. Reggie Lewis of the Boston Celtics, dead. It happens to women athletes, too, always the long and lanky ones, basketball or volleyball stars, the ones with slender fingers curling under toward their wrists, great specimens, dead. Marfan's Syndrome, a hole in the heart, a faulty valve, a heart too large, a heart hiding its flaws until the sudden failure.

There were three hospital beds turned sideways and pushed together with their side-bars down to accommodate Isaac's body. His first coherent post-operative words were spoken in a raspy whisper five days after his heart had stopped.

"Dad, I'm sorry."

"And I'm overjoyed, Isaac. You're still with us." I let go of his hand and stroked the side of his face. "Now let me go outside and get your mother."

"Wait." He squeezed my arm. In the past, he could bruise me with such pressure but now his grip was weak, child-like. "It's all over. They made that clear yesterday. No more basketball. No running. A very quiet life. What, I'm suddenly going to become a physicist? Everything we planned for is out the window."

"I never planned for any of that stuff."

He closed his eyes and seemed to drift off. I shifted my weight to get up and leave the room, but he squeezed my arm again. "The house, the car, the trips, all out the window. I can't believe it."

"It doesn't matter, Isaac. Look," I pointed to his right, "all that's out the window this morning is sunlight." I couldn't believe that these were his primary thoughts after all he'd been through, after all he'd lost for himself.

His hand fell back to the bed. He swallowed dryly. "What good is a seven-and-a-half-foot-tall non-basketball player? I've never done anything else. Never even thought about it."

"Don't exaggerate."

He blinked and looked at me closely, as though seeing me

there for the first time. "I don't think I am, Dad. This is serious, what happened to me."

"Well I think you're exaggerating. You're only seven feet five and three-quarters. Now let me go get your mother. She'll want to hear your voice."

When I brought Loretta back into the room, Isaac was asleep again. She looked at him, then back at me, her face filled with questions and worry. I bent over the bed and stroked Isaac's brow.

"What?" he whispered, opening his eyes.

"Nothing. You were dreaming, I think."

He moved his eyes back and forth. "He was here, it wasn't a dream."

I started to shake my head, contradicting him, but Isaac grew more agitated. It worried me and I thought about going out to fetch a nurse, but Loretta held me in place.

"I think I may be getting nearer to God," Isaac whispered.

"He's gotten near enough."

"I don't think so." He reached vaguely in my direction and I handed him the cup of water. "Just the outskirts, where the light turned me around."

"You can remember that?"

He nodded. "And a sound, something like a windstorm in the darkness, but filtered through a long stand of trees. I don't know." He sipped and handed back the cup. "This is something I can tell people about."

"Sure. When you're ready, maybe we can set up some kind of speaking tour."

He blinked. "I think maybe this is what I'm supposed to do, you know? Maybe it's why I'm so tall, to be closer to Him than most people."

Loretta nodded. But I didn't get what Isaac meant. He was so tall, we'd learned, because of a combination of genes and a pituitary disorder.

"Maybe," I said. "But you need to rest. You need to heal for a while before you even think about what to do next."

"This has to have happened for a reason," he whispered, closing his eyes.

"You were born with a thick wall in your heart. The pump was bad, that's the reason. You should get some sleep, there's plenty of time to talk about what you'll do."

"Nothing happens by accident," Isaac whispered. "Do you think Marius DePino was there by coincidence?"

"Yes," I said. "We're lucky his son didn't want to be an electrical engineer or they might have been watching the Gonzaga game instead."

Isaac closed his eyes. A faint hiss came from the machinery beside the bed.

Out in the hallway, Loretta took my arm and gently led me toward the waiting room at the end of the hall. We plopped down together on the brown plastic couch, sighing as one, relieved to have him talking but, I believed, a little shaken at what he was saying.

Loretta patted my arm, always a bad sign, and announced, "Well, you handled that about as badly as a man could, I would think."

e

"I'm not even sure someone who's a Jew by adoption can become a rabbi."

153

"We're reformed Jews," Loretta said. "So almost anything is possible."

I looked out the waiting room window into a parking lot where cars all neatly fitted into their diagonal slots gleamed in winter light. It seemed possible to rearrange their pattern, to shift them so they faced the other way, noses to the street instead of noses to the hospital wall, just by fluttering my eyes or twitching my pinkie.

"For some reason, I just don't like it. The idea makes me squirm."

"Who says you have to like it?" Loretta asked. Her tone wasn't particularly challenging, just curious, a gentle questioning. "I never much liked the idea of his being an athlete, myself."

"You're kidding me."

She shook her head. "So I didn't come to very many of his games. Big deal. You could skip his services, or start going to the Conservative temple, whatever." She paused, then swallowed. "The point is, George, you don't have to like what Isaac does. "

I nodded, but a person would have to be looking closely to tell. Of course she was right, I should just be glad he was still here to do anything. "Tell me something." I looked down at the cars, picking one long Lincoln and changing the angle of my head so that the reflected sun pinged off the fender like a shot. I got lost in the game of it.

"All right. But first you have to ask it."

I turned to face her. "Why do you think I'm uncomfortable with this?"

"Beats me." She got up and came over to me, putting her arms around me from behind and hugging me to her. "No it doesn't. You're terrified, my love. You're in shock. You want everything to go back to where it was two weeks ago."

I nodded, leaning back into her. "Probably right."

"And you've had enough God for a while, I think. You don't want Isaac inviting Him back into our lives any time soon."

"What if it's something else?"

"Well, then it's something else. Now why don't we go for a walk and let him sleep."

"In a minute."

"Okay, George, what is it?"

"The new house, the recliner, the trip to Rio?"

"You hate the beach."

e⌒

When we brought Isaac home two weeks later, the house immediately seemed tawdry to me. It felt too small to contain him, though he'd lived there with us all his life, and our furnishings looked shabby in a way I'd never seen before.

I'd worked hard for thirty-one years now, and this was all I had to show for it? Three decades selling people insurance, eventually opening my own office, making nice money, and I lived in a house I'm secretly embarrassed to own? We hadn't had friends over to dinner in years. I always thought it was because we were too busy, too involved with following Isaac's career or with our little projects, our routines. Now I realized it was out of shame. Who wants to bring people in here, with the faded wallpaper and dull paint and threadbare carpet? It was as if we'd stopped tending to the place five years ago, almost exactly when Isaac's potential as a basketball player revealed itself. Everyplace there was wood there were chipped surfaces, as though the house had been subject to airborne abrasion. Posters of flowers and vegetables were wavy and sagging behind their glass, windows whose seals had busted were all blurry with contained moisture, there was noise everywhere from appliances that labored to keep up. All of a sudden, I could see the place for what it was, for what it had become. An abandoned home.

While Loretta tended to Isaac upstairs, I found myself sitting in my old easy chair staring out the window. The view, what I could see of it, was east toward a commercial section of Portland. A flickering neon sign with two letters missing told people driving on the below-grade freeway that home furnishings were for sale. CAREYS FURN URE. Across the freeway, a new medical center loomed. The day seemed unnaturally dark. I turned back and listened for the sounds of my wife and son, his deep murmuring voice, her high breathy melody of comfort and devotion.

The doctors had told us that Isaac had a very good chance for a satisfactory outcome, whatever that might mean. His heart was essentially good, which I could have told them without holding it in my hands, though enlarged by years of extra pumping action. His circulation and respiration were all good, he was in great condition, under the circumstances.

It was just that he couldn't play basketball again, or engage in strenuous activity, or do much of anything he'd always done and always dreamed of doing. Perhaps what bothered me more than all this was Isaac's reaction. He seemed happy, relieved. He was still tormented by the feeling that he'd let us down, broken his promises, but with help he was getting beyond that. He seemed, in fact, gradually to have grown joyous about the new direction his life would take.

What, did I want him to be depressed? To be immobilized by despair over his losses, to be so angry that he jeopardized his recovery? No, of course not. But giddy, as though he'd been let off the hook? It was all very confusing to me.

We'd made inquiries about how Isaac could begin studying for the rabbinate because that's what he asked us to do. I'm sorry to admit that if Loretta hadn't taken over, it might not have gotten done. Neither of us—nor Isaac—had realized how many credits in philosophy and religion he'd already accumulated. Still, it would be a good five more years, provided his recovery continued apace, before he was likely to stand before a congregation of his own.

I turned back again toward the window and began to drowse. A glimmer of color erupted outside the window. At first I thought it was just the Carey Furniture sign blinking, but then it came back, a small bird darting more quickly than any point guard I'd seen on the basketball court. It was the most outrageously bright yellow, with hints of black on the wings and tail, a brilliant red head, and it zoomed across my field of vision like a flash of sunlight bright enough to cut through the barrier of the cloudy window. I thought I could even hear its hoarse call, its *pit-ik pit-ik* over the traffic sounds and the voice of the refrigerator cycling on in the kitchen. What's a western tanager doing a half mile from the Banfield Freeway, I thought. What's it doing with a red head in winter?

Then, jerking up with a start, I realized where I really wished we were, the three of us. We should be in a small house in the woods, in springtime. One of those yurts, maybe, that come pre-designed so you can assemble them yourself in the middle of your acreage. Not by an urban lake in a big house paid for by my son, but a cozy little place without many walls, located halfway between the city and the shore, precisely the kind of home I'd always dreamed of having. I had five years left for selling insurance before I was ready to retire. By then, Isaac would be finished with his studies. Could he find a congregation for himself in rural Oregon?

I stood and went over to the window. Nothing. At least, nothing in the way of yellow birds. Still, it would be nice, I thought, and turned to head upstairs to see what Loretta and Isaac might think about my dream.

THE CAGE

The path to Theo Deane's beach house was overgrown with weeds. Its entrance was hidden somewhere at the end of the gravel road where Mel Niles stopped his panel truck.

At least the man was home this time. Because here's that sleek car of his parked snug against the huckleberries and rhodies and poison oak like it's hiding from the neighbors. A Lexus, an Infiniti, an Eternity, Mel couldn't keep the names of those fancy vehicles straight. Every time you see a rig like that on Highway 101, it's this same slate-gray color.

Mel rattled around in the back of his truck for a few minutes. Bracing it on an edge, he dragged a bulky parcel over to the door, hopped out and looked around. He'd been delivering stuff to the man's house for ten months and still was never sure where the entrance to that damned path was. Mr. Deane must erase his tracks like a secret agent or something. Mel scanned the trees for the little wrinkle he'd noticed last week, not much more than a nick in the leaves. Then he looked down where it met the ground and spotted the rock shaped like a dolphin's back. There you go. Now all he had to do was lug the damn parcel two hundred yards through the woods, slip himself around a cluster of salal, cross a little bit of soft sand, heft it up six steps and knock on the door. No sweat.

Except it weighed a good sixty pounds, he thought. What now, a full-size reproduction of Candlestick Park that he can put together on the back lawn? Comes with your blustery wind, your piped-in crowd noise, smell of hot dogs. Or how about a set of bats made of brass for warming up the muscles?

Mel lifted the parcel onto his shoulder and groaned. He realized he should have used the dolly, but it was such a chore getting a dolly over the grass and sand. I know, this is a steel workout bench, some assembly required. The man had more equipment than the local gym.

At least Mel had timed it right today, caught the man when he was in. Doesn't like us to leave his parcels on the porch, doesn't want to be driving forty minutes over to the UPS office to pick them up. Bring them anytime Friday afternoon is fine, he says. And the manager actually agrees. So there's a Theo Deane corner in the office now. Some Fridays, Mel had a half-dozen things for him, three or four trips back and forth between the truck and the house like a donkey.

What the hell, it was no big deal, and every once in a while the man gave Mel a little something. Not supposed to take tips, no gifts, but Mr. Deane made it seem more like a favor on Mel's part to take the stuff from him. Two half-court tickets to a Blazers-Lakers game, for example, which was well worth the drive into Portland and back. A nice aluminum baseball bat for the little boy, hit the ball it makes a hollow ping that Mel still can't get used to hearing. A roast chicken, like Mr. Deane had accidentally cooked one too many. Last month, a set of passes to see Free Willy over at the Newport aquarium, a real killer whale that was a movie star, the kid loved it. Mel couldn't think why he'd never taken him there before. Whale swimming around in there, big smile on his face, real name of Keiko but they use a stage name when he does his films.

Mel remembered his first trip to the Deane place. It was last year, early fall, a small enough parcel to carry in one hand, probably nothing more than a housewarming gift. Wasn't long before the weekly shipments filled up a quarter of Mel's truck. That first time, he'd left the parcel by the door and was headed back to the truck when the man called out to him. Mel went around back to find him standing halfway between an enormous mound of topsoil and a good two dozen racks of sod, looking back and forth between them like he wasn't sure which one was supposed to go down first. Wind was making the rolling stretch of wild grasses look like they were waving so-long. Mel noticed the few giant coreopsis near the bluff and the occasional dune tansy and he knew exactly what was going through this man's mind. Trade this nice native look for about an eighth acre of thick, closely clipped grass, make a playground out of it. He was surprised when Theo Deane turned around with streaks of tears running down his cheeks.

Slowly, over the course of the next six months, Mel watched the place change as each new piece of equipment was installed like some kind of postmodern sculpture in this blustery garden. His Level Swing machine and his Rapid Wrist Machine, his Rocket Arm and his Pepper Net. He wondered how the man could sleep at night, all those shadows and strange howling noises when the wind blew past.

What's that noise now? Sounds like the waves turned solid back there, smacking into the wood the man has buttressing his slope. You never know what to expect when you come to Theo Deane's. A couple months ago, Mel had found him by the side of the place. Must take Fridays off there at the law firm in Portland, pretty nice deal. Had on an old-fashioned Chicago White Sox hat with twenty-some stripes running down from the button to the bill so it looked like a bird cage on his head. Had his back next to the wall of the house and dangling from the roof eaves was a baseball attached to a strap that was attached to springs that were attached to the house. He's pretending to throw the ball, concentrating so hard he couldn't hear Mel coming, and from the sweat all over his face it's obvious the man's been at this for a long time. That was his Arm Strong, a unit Mel had brought him just a week before. Didn't weigh too much. Mel had thought the parcel was maybe a collapsible fishing pole or something from the way it felt and sounded inside the packaging.

Now Mel put today's parcel down on the back porch and stretched before ringing the bell. House made of glass, just about, what they call passive solar, set right smack on the edge of the land. Got a dream house in a dream place and he's the unhappiest man Mel ever saw. Always hot in those glass houses. Mel himself was just about sweated through his shirt. Middle of February, it's sixty-six degrees, he thought. Mildest winter we've had in years. He thought he should have worn his summer uniform, stored now in the kid's closet till June maybe, the brown shorts that made him look like an old man retired to Florida.

Mel waited for Theo Deane to make his way to the front door. Always something. Either he's in the shower, middle of the

afternoon, or he's in the back room daydreaming, or he's off some-
where working out. Then it's *Just a minute, Mel.* Name that tune.

Nothing doing. So Mel rang again, then heard the voice rid-
ing on the breeze: "I'm out back."

Well, fine and dandy, you're out back. I'm not about to drag
this parcel to you. Mel left it leaning against the wall and walked
around the house.

Theo Deane was in a cage. A long, low cage, its mesh thick
enough to darken what—all was inside. The cage stretched most
of the way across his back yard, a good seventy feet long, held in
place by three blue metal braces front, rear, and middle. At one
end, there was a machine spitting baseballs out of a hole dead-
center. At the other end, there was Theo Deane—in a shabby gray
sweat suit and this time a battered old navy blue New York Yankees
cap—swatting at the baseballs and grunting each time he swung.

"Just a minute, Mel. There's five," then he shut up while an-
other pitch came and he swung and grunted. "More balls in there
before," another pitch, another swing and grunt. "I can get out
of here."

Mel. Calls me Mel and wants me to call him Theo. Hard to
do that because the man just seems like a Mr. Deane, not a Theo.
What kind of name is Theo, anyway, Greek? Theo, the God of
Parcels. Apparently, he was once called Teddy, which must have
been a very long time ago because he's got about as much Teddy
in him now as Mel has Bunny, which used to be his nickname
till he got old enough to put a stop to it. Teddy Deane, played a
season-and-a-half in the big leagues, a real hot-shot, a Yankee in
pinstripes, till he took a pitch in the face, busted up his eyesocket.
Mel had looked him up in the boy's *Baseball Encyclopedia,* one

skinny little entry with huge numbers, led the league in this and that, and then he's gone.

He sure hit the last pitch on the sweet spot. Jesus, Mel thought, that one sounded like a gunshot. Sees well enough now.

Theo Deane came out of the cage, wiping his face with a towel that had been dangling from the door. Towel had Brooklyn Dodgers written on it in fancy blue script. Huh, not much loyalty in the man.

"Sorry about that, Mel." Theo smiled and led them back around the front of the house, taking the porch steps two at a time. "Had to finish my hundred swings." Mel followed, just wanting to get the man's John Hancock and get out of there. Plenty of stops to make yet.

"There it is," Theo said as he touched the parcel. "I've been waiting for this."

Man, look at this guy. We're probably the same height and weight but he looks four inches taller and thirty pounds lighter. Not a crease anywhere—the face, the neck, even the sweat clothes he's got on and you know he's been working out in them for a while. How's a guy get to look like that?

Mel handed him the brown plastic gizmo and magic pen for a signature. Not supposed to ask customers what's inside a parcel, but curiosity was killing him. As was his neck, carrying the thing.

Theo finished signing and looked up. He smiled as he read Mel's face. "It's a Solo Socker, Mel. No home's complete without one."

Mel nodded like he knew what the hell the man was talking about, pursing his lips, narrowing his eyes. Then he turned around to leave. "See you next time, Mr. Deane."

"Theo."

"Right. Well, you have a good week, Theo."

Serves me right, Mel thought as he walked past the salal. Serves me fine, wondering what's inside.

A Solo Socker. What the hell is that, some kind of code words? I'm supposed to know what he's talking about? Maybe the man is a spy after all. He sure is a solo socker, Mel thought, no friends that I ever see. Except there was that one lady back in the fall, was here a couple times, had those legs on her so she didn't need stairs to get up into the man's loft. Ol' Theo and this one could look each another in the eye, she must have been a steady six-two. Had that one blue eye and the other brown, the strangest looking woman Mel ever had seen. Peeking out at him from under a thick strand of copper colored hair. Strange, but what's the word he was looking for? Alluring, that's it. Just about had Mel hypnotized when she was talking about these scallops she wanted to cook.

But she's gone now. Which is probably why he's out there in the cage. A solo socker, that's how the man struck Mel from the get-go.

The next week, Mel was back there with three parcels, each one as big as the Solo Socker. Pretty soon, the man's going to have to buy the land next door just to house all this equipment. That, or start throwing some of the older stuff over the edge. Maybe he's got one of those underground bunkers somewhere for stuff he isn't using.

When Mel returned with the final parcel, Theo Deane was waiting with a glass of lemonade. Make that a vat of lemonade.

Mel wondered how long he was supposed to hang around there trying to drink the whole thing down.

"Come around back with me a minute," Theo said. "You can help me with something."

Mel walked with him, but hung back a little. Just what he needed, start helping customers assemble the junk he brings them. Take him three days just to deliver one day's worth of parcels. Mel had a full afternoon's work left and couldn't be playing games here.

"Don't worry, this won't take five minutes."

Damn, the man can read my mind. Spooky. Mel tried to drink and walk at the same time, to keep up with Theo, but he had to stop before any more lemonade ended up on his shirt.

"Come on in here with me," Theo said, unlatching the cage's door, which was just a frame of metal poles strung with the same dark netting as the rest of the cage. Mel thought, he wants me to go in the cage with him?

"Man, I haven't hit a pitched ball in years."

"That's okay, Mel. All I want is for you to adjust the pitching machine while I stand in the box. Can't get the damn thing set right. It hasn't thrown me a strike all day."

"I don't have a screwdriver on me."

Theo laughed. "Just tilt the head of the thing a notch or two, once we get going."

So Theo stood beside the official home plate he'd nailed at one end of the cage and Mel, putting his drink down on the soft grass and sure it was going to topple over, stood by the pitching machine at the other end. He did not like the light in here, if you could call this light. Plenty bright enough to see, no doubt about that, but stripped of its warmth or something. Taupe, he thought.

The light in here's taupe. Or dead, maybe that's closer.

"They've got machines now that can throw curve balls," Theo said as he waggled the bat toward Mel. "I just ordered one."

Great, Mel thought, and it probably weighs eight hundred pounds.

"Don't worry, it's light as a feather. All right, see if you can move the head on that down about a half-inch."

Mel touched the top of the machine, which moved fractionally and spit out a ball. It looked like Theo was going to swing. Mel threw himself to the ground, remembering the rifle shot sound he'd heard last week.

"Jesus, Mel, I wouldn't hit the ball with you in here. Relax."

You relax, Mel thought. He dusted off some stray grass and took his position again, adjusting the machine according to Theo's directions and watching him like he'd watch a panther in the wild.

"Next week," Theo said, "I should be able to tell. Once I get that new machine."

After his injury, Theo had tried to come back, tried to play again for the Yankees. But he couldn't see well enough to track the ball's flight and got dizzy whenever a pitch curved. He couldn't catch either, the ball caroming off the tip or heel of his mitt. Soon, his left eye began developing an early form of cataracts. He went through a lengthy course of laser surgeries, but his vision simply never came around. For half a year, he couldn't stand up for more than twenty minutes at a time without losing his balance.

It took six months to admit that he was finished as a baseball player. The doctors were the first to say so. Even the Yankees said so before Theo did. One night in May, when the next season was already well underway, he called his brother Conor and said, "I guess I can afford law school now."

In three years, he'd established his practice in Portland, a city he loved for its setting and its easy style, what the magazines called livability. The opposite of New York. He even liked its rain. Portlanders liked that he was a former ballplayer, but didn't hound him on the streets, reserving that for their beloved basketball players. And it was the right place to practice environmental law. Soon Conor had moved up from San Francisco and they were practicing together. But in the last couple of years, Theo had begun losing focus. He turned more and more work over to Conor and the staff, tried fewer cases, and began to plan his comeback. He hadn't been in court in seventeen months. He was thirty-two. It was now or never. Conor told him he was nuts and threatened to move back south.

When they were finished adjusting the machine, Theo led Mel back around to the front of the house. Mel looked at his watch. He would have to drive like a maniac to get back on schedule.

"I won't keep you but a minute longer, Mel. You ever play any ball?"

Oh wonderful, now he wants to reminisce. I could be here till Sunday. Mel didn't think the man really wanted to know about his story, so he said, "Just some high school hoops."

Theo halted as if walking into a wall. "Wait a minute, I recognize that tone of voice."

"What?" Mel played back what he'd just said. "What tone of voice are you talking about?"

"*Just some high school hoops.* Come on, tell me more about your high school hoops."

"That," Mel snorted. "Well, it was fun while it lasted. This was in Portland, eighty-three, eighty-four. We had a run at the state finals two years straight and I got some college offers. Took a full ride to Oregon State, man, the Beavers. But then I tore up my knee freshman year, the scholarship went away and I finished my degree at the community college back home while I worked hauling freight around. All I wanted to do was move out here to the coast. Like I said, just some high school hoops."

"So what did you do with it?"

"Do with what?"

"I don't know, your desire to play, all that energy." Theo waved his arm vaguely in the direction of the ocean. "The drive."

Mel shook his head. "I don't even watch it on TV, hardly. I got a life to live, wife and kids, work. What do I want to do with playing hoops? Tear up my knee again and lose my job?"

"You have a court at the house, though, am I right? The nice backboard and a rim with a net."

"What for?"

"You're kidding me."

Mel shook his head again.

"You can just let it go?"

"Let it go? I never had a hold of it. Look, I got to get back to work, Mr. Deane. Thanks for the lemonade."

"Theo," he took the glass from Mel. "Do me a favor and call me Theo, all right? Now what about your son?"

Mel studied the man's face. Don't go near that, Mr. Deane. "What about him?"

"Aren't you going to teach him?"

Mel chuckled. "Lee takes after his mother. Winter, he wants to be a wrestler."

After Mel left, Theo went back into the batting cage and be-
gan rounding up balls. He loaded them into the machine's auto-
feeder, set the speed ten m.p.h. slower, and trotted to the far end.
Picking up the bat, he quickly set himself and crouched.

He hated the way it sounded in here. The slightest wind whis-
tled when it passed through the cage's netting. The occasional sea
gull circling above him, bugling for food, sounded like a besot-
ted Bronx heckler. No matter how much oil he slathered on the
machine, the gears clacked and clattered as it loaded each ball
and he could always tell when the pitch was about to come. This
did not make for good practice. The light seemed strange too, as
though stained by the sand and pollen that gathered in the netting.
He could use some stadium-quality lights, though the neighbors
might not appreciate them. Lights and maybe one of those adjust-
able tees that help you shorten your stroke, and a recording of
ballpark sounds—the vendors, the chatter and cheers, throw in a
few nasty jeers. *Hey Deane, go back to court, ya bum.*

He was just being too sensitive, having trouble concentrating.
Bear down and hit, Deane.

He pulled the first pitch hard into the netting at his right. That
would have landed in the dugout, he thought, and scattered the
whole team. In the back of the baseball magazines he'd been read-
ing, where the equipment and other items for sale are featured, they
had personals ads now too. Russian ladies who wanted to meet
ballplayers or fans or anybody in America who ever ate a peanut.
Asian girls who loved to please. Hey, baseball was huge in Japan,
maybe one of those girls knew how to pitch the split-finger fastball.

Theo waited on the next pitch and lined it into the net to his left. Better. A double over third. His mind was getting clearer now. He hit the next pitch into the screen in front of the pitching machine. Take that, sucker. It wasn't till the sixth ball that he hit one really right, a rising liner into the corner of the cage, a sure gapper, three bases in the old days when he had his speed. Well, he still could run, maybe not as fast but for much longer than when he was playing. He was in better shape now and every bit as strong, he thought.

Right, and I know the law better too. But that and all my practice here is not likely to get me into a Yankee uniform again. Maybe the Devil Rays, though, new team looking for a crowd-pleaser. Theo wondered if he could talk Conor into being his agent, make a couple calls.

When the machine was empty, Theo rounded up the balls, loaded them, and shut the machine down. He left the cage, walking toward the house while he slipped off his batting gloves and put them in his rear pocket. His original plan had been to stay in Portland this weekend, since he had a dinner appointment scheduled for Sunday afternoon. It was a lot of driving for just one full day of practice, but he couldn't bear to be away from it anymore. Besides, he didn't mind the road between Portland and the coast, especially this time of year when there was less traffic and the evergreens were a dark tunnel at the summit of the Coast Range.

Theo moved the three parcels into his shed and hefted the big parcel that Mel had brought last week. He carried it around to the back, tore it open and spread the flaps on the grass. Just as he'd thought. Solo Sockers came in about twenty pieces banded together without instructions. That's why he hadn't touched it all week. He started sorting them. They were mostly interlocking tubes and brackets, in schoolhouse red, with one rectangle of mesh about the size of a twin bedsheet, a length of elasticized cord and a cheap baseball. Simple enough. But something was off, he wasn't sure what.

As Theo went inside for a screwdriver, the sudden warmth of the house made him realize what the problem was. Aerodynamics. In the harsh coast winds and storms, he'd need something to anchor his Solo Socker or the whole unit would end up on Highway 101.

He stopped long enough to pour himself a glass of Merlot, took a sip, then left it on the counter as he went to the shed for a bucket. He spent the next ten minutes gathering up small stones, working his way along the path to the gravel lot by the road. In the woods, footsteps crunched over fallen leaves and twigs, probably a hungry raccoon or stray cat.

Theo remembered that he hadn't stopped to pick anything up for dinner. So he would have to go out, driving another twenty minutes each way to the nearest restaurant. Now he realized the afternoon was cooling fast. Things felt like they were beginning to crowd up on him. It would be sunset soon and Theo tried never to miss a coast sunset. Every weekend while he was at the beach, he stopped whatever he was doing, walked to the edge of the bluff, sat with his back against the smooth driftwood lair he'd assembled the first week he'd moved in, and thought of nothing but the slow descent of the sun. Even when it was too cloudy to see the sun, which it often was, Theo went to the bluff and watched anyway. Which meant he'd better hustle.

Coming back behind the house again, he filled the tubes that would comprise the Solo Socker's base with stones before fitting them together and locking them in place with brackets. If this didn't work, he'd fix up some metal clamps and spike them into the ground, holding the thing in place like a tent in an alpine meadow.

It took a while to get the elastic cord attached properly to the top and bottom braces, but when he had it together right the baseball settled in the heart of his strike zone and Theo smiled. Looked pretty good. He could work on his stroke first thing in the morning, practice keeping the swing short. The cases he was working on back in Portland could wait. Hell, the law always waits, at least environmental law does. Motions and countermotions, like the movement of the tides. There was no rush for anything. He slapped the ball once with his hand to test the cord's tension, went inside, picked up his wine and headed for the driftwood.

Mel got home about a half hour late. He'd speeded things up after leaving the man's place, but not enough to break even. He knew Sandra was going to be a bit testy, Friday night and he's holding things up.

His son was sitting on the floor of the living room, back pressed against the sofa, watching television. His hat was on backwards, of course, and he was squeezing two hand grips, strengthening himself up while he watched his show.

Mel followed the sound of clattering cookware and found Sandra in the kitchen, nodding to herself. Great, either she's singing, which is a good sign, or she's agreeing with herself that marrying Mel Niles was as dumb as her father always said, which was not such a good sign.

He walked over and slipped his arms around her waist, drawing Sandra close, nuzzling her neck, kissing behind her ear the way she liked. "Sorry, baby, I'm a little late. I'll make it up to you."

Then he left the room before she had a chance to say anything harsh. He wandered into the living room and sat on the sofa so that his legs hung next to Lee's left shoulder.

"How was school, my man?"

Lee actually muted the television. That was a first. Mel hoped the boy wasn't in some kind of trouble.

"No problem," Lee said. "I made weight, so I go varsity tomorrow against Otis."

"I didn't know Otis had a high school."

"Otis Levingston, Pop. Third in state last year."

Mel nodded. "What time you on?"

"Could be five, five-thirty."

Mel had missed the last three times his son wrestled. They weren't going to talk about that, exactly, but he knew it would be good for him to be there tomorrow. He wanted to, he really did, and it was a Saturday meet too, pretty rare, a tournament. But he was so damn tired.

Hell with that. Mel went upstairs to change. He would go to sleep early, sleep late, whatever it took, but he'd be there when Lee tangled with this Otis kid. Bank on it.

He took off his watch and dangled its band from the raised, golden arm of the figure on his state basketball championship trophy. He undressed and took a quick shower. Then he came downstairs wearing his old tan chinos and the faded gray tee-shirt that said Benson High School Basketball, proud that he could still fit in the thing.

Sandra was setting the kitchen table. Mel took her in his arms again and kissed her lips, taking the silverware out of her hand while he did, and gently nudging her toward the chair that she always sat in for her meals.

"What's with you?" Sandra asked.

Mel smiled at her. He took care to put the knives, forks and spoons just where she liked them, all facing the right way, each utensil where it was supposed to go.

THE PEANUT VENDOR

My name is Randall Alvin Gilliam and I have always hated nick-names. In Vietnam they called me RAG because of my initials. They did, that is, till I told them RAG was just one F away from FRAG, and smiled that roll-eyed leer Daddy used to call my pre-exorcism look. Later, when I accidentally took out a group of my own guys at the river near Tam Ky and got brought up on charges, that little joke came back to haunt me.

Anyway, now I call myself Mr. Nutz. Got it printed on my tee-shirt and across the crown of my cap. For twenty years I've been selling peanuts in the Seattle Kingdome. What am I going to do, go around as Goober?

The day they opened the Kingdome for baseball, I was there working the aisles. What a place. A baseball stadium with a dome is like an Italian church without one. A sacrilege, I know that. The Kingdome is surreal enough to remind me of the old days near Tam Ky. It isn't the goofy green carpet the team plays on or even the stillness of the air, like in Vietnam before an afternoon rain. It's the noise, the racket of human and mechanical sounds that go haywire at all the wrong times. It's also the absence of dark or hush or breeze, and sudden explosions like incoming fire when a Mariner hits a home run. It's the lack of sea smell even though we're right by the sea, and sweat and explosives lingering so heavy in the air. It's a zone cut off from everything else. Man, I tell you the ballpark gets me juiced.

I plan to be there the day they close this place and move a few yards down the parking lot to that new Safeco Field. Cal Ripken Jr. doesn't have a thing on Mr. Nutz. I haven't missed a game since Ripken was still in high school.

If the boss didn't require it, I wouldn't sell one bag of peanuts before the fifth inning. Late-inning stuff is what interests me, when the fans have already gorged themselves on hot dogs and sausages and malts, when they've gone through a few beers and those alleged nachos and the neon snow cones. If a man can sell peanuts then, he's a true wizard. It's like being a relief pitcher: Let me play when the challenge is stiffest.

People think the key to selling food at a ballpark is the spiel. Gravel up the voice, get a spiffy slogan like "HOT peanuts for the HOT corner" while you're vending over on the third base side. Wrong. Baseball is a boring game most of the time, that's what I have come to believe, and so the key is to put on a show. Not too obviously, but be distracting nevertheless, like a small itch. I know that's what they call counterintuitive nowadays, but it works for me.

I stroll up the aisles growling, "See Mr. Nutz! Ah nuts!" and my trademark is throwing the bag as far and accurately as possible. The farther the better. My peanuts come wrapped in fist-size foil packets ideal for throwing and I do believe I can hit a patron from just about any point in the park. Despite the thick strap around my shoulders and the bulky tray across my middle, there's nothing I can't do with a bag of nuts when I put my mind to it. Once, the highlight of my career to date, August 1986, I tossed a bag from the field boxes to a fan standing way up in the second deck. It wasn't the distance that mattered—I've tossed bags five times as far—but the transaction occurred at exactly the moment a foul ball was hit in the same direction. The fan looked up for an instant as people rose all around him, and I could see him decide to catch the bag of nuts thrown by Randall Alvin Gilliam rather than the foul ball hit by the mighty José Canseco. Amazing as that may sound, it happened, and the stadium erupted, fans roaring their approval. I'll never forget.

All year, I've been stretching out the distance, taking a fan's order and then backing up, backing up, teasing the crowd, an impossible distance, but then tossing it, sometimes behind my back, sometimes through my legs, sometimes, if the distance is great enough, overhand like a shortstop, and then I walk all the way back to collect my money to the cheers of the crowd. May seem like a waste of time and energy, but all you need to see is my take at the end of a game to realize how effective I am.

It's bottom of the sixth inning now and I've gone through four loads of nuts already. Must be the Saturday hungries, because I haven't even been trying hard yet. A few behind-the-backs, one through the legs because the fan was a little kid and I knew he'd like that, and for the pretty red-headed lady with her pony tail sticking through the adjustable band behind her Mariners cap, a cross-aisle lob like a hand-grenade. You wouldn't believe how many people will give me two bucks and tell me to keep the change, a thirty-three percent tip and what does that tell you?

All right, I'm a bit of a genius. I'm an artist. Sometimes the things I come up with scare me, they're so brilliant.

When this idea comes to me, I almost drop my loaded tray of nuts and start dancing. Can it be done, I wonder? Here I stand behind the Mariners' dugout making change and there's a fellow sitting behind the visitors' dugout already waving at me from across the field. Flailing away like I'm his long-lost son. Well, Pops, how about it, think I can throw you your peanuts from here? Clear across the diamond. Maybe the manager kicking his legs back and forth while he sits in the dugout will just have to offer me a contract when he sees this, who knows?

I wave back. I lift up a bag so he can see the silver foil glitter and then I point at him so he'll know we have a deal. Nothing worse than tossing a fan nuts and then he says he isn't paying because he never asked me for them.

People sitting around me notice what's going on right away. These are the expensive seats. Folks sitting here generally don't like to watch the action on the field anyway. Always looking around, always looking for something to buy. They're with me. Guy here to my left is leaning across the aisle, probably setting up a little wager with him. Bet on Mr. Nutz, buddy.

Now his friend gets up to leave the playing area. Probably wants something more exotic to eat than peanuts. I made him hungry, but he thinks pizza instead. Anyway, he's about to miss something special, like those fans back during the 1954 World Series who went to the can and missed Willie Mays' famous catch.

This is perfect timing. Next inning we've got the seventh-inning stretch, everybody stands up and sings "Take Me Out to the Ball Game," which ruins my business for the next twenty minutes.

So now is the moment. I put down my tray, flip a bag of nuts hand to hand, toss it around my back once and catch it, through the legs, I'm like a Harlem Globetrotter, magic touch. Then I launch it.

Immediately I can see something's wrong. The fan across the field has sat down. What's the matter with him? And now here comes the manager out of the visitors' dugout, he's going to go talk to his pitcher, all the action's stopped, and I can see right away that my bag of nuts isn't going to make it across the field. Not even close. Fact is, it could even hit the manager in the head if he doesn't hurry up.

Man, I can't look. I'm out of here.

There was so much noise all of a sudden, I didn't have time to think. Off to my right, couldn't be more than fifty yards, but it was too dark to see. After Tam Ky, we understood that anything could happen, man, that whole seaside village had just turned into a wave of fire. So we needed to quit thinking and just do. Which I did. Figured I'd tossed the grenade far enough. None of our guys were supposed to be down by the water anyway.

They're laughing. They're showing replays on the big screen, for God's sake. The mascot, that ridiculous Moose in a uniform, is coming over to shake my hand. Mr. Nutz. Oh, man, I am finished. Finished again.

THE FIGHTS

What a fall, what a winter. First Roosevelt was reelected, trouncing Landon by eleven million votes. This was the best the Republicans could come up with, the Governor of Kansas? Then sit-down strikes spread like some kind of influenza out of Flint and soon half a million people were striking auto plants across the country. The Germans were still up to no good, building the Siegfried Line, and you had a rebellion in Spain, and all of a sudden there was war between China and Japan. The world was a mess. It was forty-five below zero someplace in California, fifty below in Nevada. Even a subway World Series between the Giants and Yanks had done nothing to ease Murray Perlman's nerves.

Which were shot anyway, after Sally O'Day.

He was not a particularly nervous man and he was not at all accustomed to following world news. But his time with Sally O'Day had changed Murray. She could fill an entire evening with talk about a guy named Gandhi teaching people to farm in India or about American troops pulling out of Haiti, which Murray never knew there were troops in. Starting when Sally slid into the car beside him, she'd carry on while they drove through the boroughs, sat in some night club for a few drinks, walked through a park or Coney Island, ate a dozen cherrystones. Sally couldn't believe Murray didn't know where Ireland was exactly, or what her problem was with England. He'd felt proud of himself one night when, having accidently listened to the news on the market's radio that afternoon, he mentioned that King George V had died. Sally flushed in an instant and began a string of curses against the king's soul that took Murray's breath away. It was like sticking your hand in a coop without paying attention. You could get nipped bad. Soon he began to read more than the sports section of the morning newspaper. He felt like he was back in school again.

Murray met Sally O'Day at the fights in Rahway, January of 1934. God, was it really three years ago already? He'd wanted to marry her by Valentine's Day, and had even considered proposing in late September. But first he would have to bring her home to meet his parents and Murray hadn't quite figured out how to walk into the apartment in Brooklyn and announce to Emanuel and Sophia Perlman that this blond Irish girl was his intended. He could just see his mother, whose rhomboid face had yet to be cracked by any lines of habitual smiling, poised with utensils in mid-air, staring at his father, the would-be rabbi, the son of three generations of rabbis, who would put his knife and fork down with a careful clatter against the flowered Shabbos china, look up at them from under unruly brows—the only disorderly things in his life—close his eyes, and with perhaps the hint of a smile say, "I don't believe so."

Murray would never forget that first night at the fights, when Sally's face floated up over her brother's shoulder like the moon. Murray's best friend, Si Sloan, was still boxing then, though his loss to Carnera had ended any hopes he might have had for a championship bout. Of course Murray was in Si's corner. It was snowing lightly, so they'd already accepted the fact that there would be fewer than fifty people in the gym. Si was scheduled for ten rounds against a guy from Queens called Matthew O'Day. *Come to Rahway and See Simon "The Giant" Sloan Fight Matty "The Kid" O'Day on Tuesday the 21st!*

That evening at 5:00, Si came down to Murray's market dressed in his usual fight-night leopard-skin coat that reached to his ankles. Despite his size, Si moved with the true grace of a great cat, especially when he wore the long coat. He'd walked through the doors without a sound and suddenly loomed over Florence Teitelbaum, who was waiting for her Tuesday pullets. She shrieked, leaping aside and losing her balance. She banged into the coops lining the market wall and was so upset that Murray gave her the birds for free.

Modulating his bass voice still lower, so that he seemed to be growling instead of speaking, Si apologized. "I'll pay you back out of the winnings tonight, Mashie."

Murray closed the market an hour early, throwing his bloody apron onto a pile in the back room, by the plucking machines whose odor he no longer smelled. "What the hell," he said, "you'll scare off all my customers anyway."

"You mean the weather will."

"Shaddup. Cold nights, people need their poultry even more."

As they drove out to Queens, the snow began. Murray flicked on the windshield wipers.

"It's a sign," Si murmured.

"Yeah, right. A sign we're gonna make about twelve bucks tonight."

"Wish I could have another shot at Carnera."

"He's fighting Loughran down in Miami in a couple months. Which it shoulda been you, a rematch. We could swing over to Havana after, have a nice little time, get some fresh cigars."

"What have I got, another couple years as a fighter, the most? I'm about old enough to be Matthew O'Day's father, for Christ's sake. When boxing's over I'm not even sure I could be in the poultry business. I'm through with blood."

"Look: A, you're gonna be in the wholesale end, not retail. So B, you don't have to put your hands on a bird if you don't want to because C, you're gonna be an owner just like they agreed when you made that Carnera deal in the first place. So stop worrying. You fight this kid tonight and be ready to rock him back to sunny Ireland or wherever the hell they got him from."

"We'll see about this *owner* business. Those boys we dealt with, sometimes they have very short memories."

"I don't," Murray said. He took out a long Havana cigar and began to unwrap it with one hand. "There's a guy comes into the market every month or so. I mention it to him from time to time, refresh his memory.

If there was a part of being in Si's corner that Murray hated, it was when they first entered the ring. He didn't mind sitting in the dressing room trying to keep Si's spirits up, taping his enormous hands, rubbing down his shoulders. He didn't mind tromping down the aisle to the ring and hearing the loudmouths blather. But once they were there, with his short arms Murray could barely hold the ropes apart far enough for Si to squeeze through, and then they had to stand together for the introductions, Si looming over him. Murray was much happier once the referee had told everybody the rules and sent them back to their corners. He got Si seated on the stool, spun out to straddle the post, and put his chin on Si's shoulder so they could both look across the ring at Matthew O'Day and glower.

That's when he saw her. Sally's head of pale curls just rose into view, shrouded in smoke, as she stood to cheer her brother on. She was the most beautiful woman Murray had ever seen, despite a nose that looked as though it had been broken more often than her brother's and a thick scar that crossed her face—now crimson with excitement—running from the corner of her left eye to the center of her chin.

During the fight, Sally O'Day made Murray sloppy with his sponges and water. He conked Si's jaw with the spit bucket between rounds four and five. Drenched by a spray of sweat and spit and blood and water, forgetting to holler either encouragement or advice in Si's ear, smiling incongruously as the two fighters traded blows about six inches from his face, Murray was as dazed as Matthew ("Come on, Matty") O'Day by the time Si put the kid down for good in the eighth.

"Great fight," he managed to say over the ringing of the bell.

"You were there?" Si answered. He leaned back against the ropes in his corner, waiting for the formal announcement of his victory, trying to get his breath back to normal.

"Come on, it was me that kept you together after the third round, which he almost had you with that uppercut."

While Murray untied the gloves, Si said, "In case you couldn't tell, that girl over there's no Jew. And your name's Murray, not Seamus."

"Ayyy, what makes you think I was looking at some girl?

Everything I was looking at was between the ropes, which we had a fight going on."

Si snorted. "Mashie, I've known you since the third grade. Only thing is, she's not as bosomy as you like."

After the referee had held Si's hand up and the gym began to clear, Murray dallied in the corner, taking a long time to gather up their things. He watched Sally comforting her brother, helping him down from the ring, gazing after him as he made his way to the dressing room.

"Fought a nice fight, your brother."

She turned slowly, not seeing him at first, tracking the voice like a wary animal. "How big's your friend there, three-fifty, four hundred pounds? Fucking mismatch."

Sally liked Marx Brothers' movies and Charlie Chaplin. She enjoyed film biographies—Louis Pasteur, Emile Zola. They went to see *Captains Courageous* and she swore Murray looked a lot like Spencer Tracy. In the first six months with her, Murray saw more films than he'd seen before in his whole life. She'd slouch beside him in the theater, legs over the seat in front of her, an arm around his shoulders, and munch on shelled peanuts smuggled in her purse. They'd pass a flask of whiskey back and forth. She was so slender, Murray couldn't account for her huge presence beside him. Her longshoreman's laugh filled the loge, as did her sobs, and she seemed to envelop him.

She loved to ride horses with him in Prospect Park. Sunday mornings, they'd meet at Kinsella's, a diner in her neighborhood, wolfing down their eggs-over-easy and fried potatoes so they could be at the stables early. Once, Murray reached across the table to dab at some yolk that was congealing in the scar near Sally's chin. She slapped his hand away hard, making him knock over her glass of grapefruit juice.

Before he could think—it had all happened so fast and the mood at their table had mutated so suddenly—Murray's hand had formed a fist and he was about to launch a right cross at her. He froze. They stared at one another, hands still in the air, and didn't speak.

Finally, Sally looked down and said, "It was an accident, see. My father, you'll meet him someday, he was drunk. We went over the side of this road up near Tarrytown. There was a lot of glass. He wasn't scratched."

"Look, you know?" He gazed down at his hand as if it belonged to the table rather than to him. "I wouldn't really hit you. I mean, I don't know."

"It's all right." In a moment, she looked back up at him. "At least you didn't follow through."

Sally wanted to ride a different horse each week. Murray, who always rode the same thick palomino named Zev, after the 1923 Derby winner, thought Sally lacked discipline on a horse. But he liked to watch her gallop and to see the smile it brought to her face, the only time smiling actually transversed her scar to include the entire face.

One spring morning while they were cantering, she bolted away from him. She was on a flashy bay named Burnt Sienna, who was known around the stables as headstrong. Murray, still sluggish from breakfast, was slow to react and Zev was confused beneath him. It was five or six seconds before they took off after her. He could see that Sally was almost out of control, maybe because of the wind, maybe because she was distracted by how far ahead she'd gotten. Although it was invisible from where she was, he knew she was nearing where the path would plunge downhill and suddenly cross a street heavy with church-going traffic. This was no place to be galloping. There were signs, but she wasn't likely to read them and it was useless to call to her. He began to catch up. Then Murray saw that the wind was toying with her hat. She straightened in her saddle and Burnt Sienna slowed slightly. Murray urged Zev on and was close enough behind her that, when the hat blew off, he leaned down and snatched it out of the air.

"My hero," Sally said, laughing as they came to a stop.

Murray put her hat on his head, where it just managed to cover his bald spot like a yarmulke. Their horses were edgy, wanting to run again. Sally reached down to stroke Burnt Sienna's neck. Murray was sure she'd be bucked off in an instant, but he'd learned by now not to try controlling her horse. He kept his hands to himself.

"I like you better without the hat," he said.

"Murray Perlman, what a bold thing to say to a lass. And on a Sunday, no less."

They began to walk along the trail again, headed down toward the street. "I think you'd better stay with me," Murray said.

"And why should I do that?"

"I know these paths. And besides, you're a little wild."

They reached the street, holding up traffic while they clopped across. Then she turned to fix him with a smile. "Exactly, my brilliant. And wild is why you'll keep chasing me."

She took off again. Murray laughed out loud. Before he went after her, he tucked Sally's hat into his belt.

A little over a year later, Si had a bout scheduled for April 12, a true Friday night fight, the best card he'd been on since Carnera. They'd have to drive to Philly and stay overnight, but it would be worth doing. Si was actually smiling again, at least once in a while, and talking about putting enough money aside to buy a little place near Sheepshead Bay.

Training was the worst time for Murray because he had to squeeze roadwork in before he opened the market at 5:30 in the morning. Now that he was seeing Sally in the evenings, Murray was always exhausted when he met Si at 4:30 in the park.

Si's voice rumbled out of the depths of his toweled, hooded head. "You don't look so good."

"And you look like a peccadillo in that getup, so don't give me any crap."

Murray handed Si two socks filled with weights. They began to jog along the same bridle paths Murray had ridden with Sally. Every quarter mile or so, Si would throw a few punches at the air, turn to dance a few steps backwards, then spin forward again, still jabbing away. Murray would run loops around him during those interludes, chanting *keep it up keep it up*.

"So what's new with you and Our Lady of the O'Days?" Si said.

"Let's talk strategy, okay?"

"You're not supposed to have strategies in love."

"I'm talking about your fight, Simon. You know, the reason we're out here in the middle of the night, which I should be asleep right now."

Si was moving backwards again, with Murray circling him

and feinting punches of his own. "I mean it, Mashie. What's going on with you two? It's been what, sixteen months? I haven't met her yet."

"Keep it up keep it up. Jesus, nothing's going on. We just keep to ourselves. I haven't met none of her friends and none of her family, myself."

"That's not technically true. If I recall, there was her brother, young 'Look Out Matty,' around that first night. Hey, maybe that's it. He probably doesn't like the friends you keep. She neither. Is that why I haven't had the honor?"

"What're you talking about? Come on, let's do the miles, I gotta get to the market."

Si reached out to grab Murray's arm and they stopped jogging. "What's going on? Why don't I meet her? Why don't your parents? Why don't you meet her people? And why the hell did you just call me Simon? I've known you since we were nine and that's the first time you ever called me Simon. What did you do, knock her up?"

"Shaddup." Murray turned away, hunched his shoulders, jogged in place. "It's just, well, I . . . . Jesus, Si, we got some road-work to do."

The night before the fight, April the 11th, Murray closed the market early again. He scrubbed his hands in the back room, but there wasn't any soap left and he couldn't get all the dried blood out from under his fingernails. He knew he smelled like gizzards. Good thing he wasn't going to see Sally tonight. And tomorrow he didn't want to think about. Which there was no choice, he had to leave it up to Teddy Phillips to run the place tomorrow while they were in Philly, to open it on time, to keep it open all day. And it was Friday, no less! Shabbos, when all his best customers would come in for their Sabbath chickens.

He walked up the street without seeing anything, all his concentration focused inward on the horror of what would probably happen tomorrow in the market. The floor would be filthy, Teddy would forget to put down fresh sawdust during the day and there would be bloody lumps all over the floor, he'd be rude to women who weren't pretty enough, and the birds would not be properly drained. So when he reached the car, sunk in a morbid despair, Murray was astonished to find Sally leaning against the driver's door.

"What's this?" he said.

"This is a valise."

"That's not what I mean. What're you doing here?"

Sally's eyes narrowed. "Don't be ridiculous, all right? Just open the door, I don't want to stand here like this."

"Look, we're going to Philly, you know that. Si's got a fight, which we sleep in some cheap joint afterwards and then come home."

"I know all that. Jeez, I thought you'd be happy I was coming with you."

"It's no place for a girl."

She put her elbows on the hood of the car and stared at him. Murray held her stare.

"I grew up around fights, Murray. Maybe you remember where we first met? And I'm not only coming to Philly, I'm coming to that holy chicken market of yours when we get back. I want to see you in your real world."

Murray was shaking his head as he unwrapped a cigar and bit off the end. He wouldn't look at her.

"Besides," he said.

"Besides, nothing. It's time I got to know Si as somebody other than a gorilla who tore my Matty apart."

He walked around the car, unlocked the passenger door and waited for Sally to get in. Then he squatted down and leaned in next to her. "Si and me, we do a certain way before he fights. Which we haven't done it any different for maybe ten years."

"Like what?"

"Okay, just tell me this. Where you gonna sleep?"

"Why, does Si usually sleep in the bed with you?"

When they stopped in front of Si's apartment, he was just locking the door. His enormous, leopard-skinned back filled the doorway. He turned, grinning, with two cigars stuck in his mouth and pointing skyward. When he saw Sally next to Murray in the car, both cigars dove toward the ground.

He tried to climb into the backseat and couldn't make it, so he stepped out, turned around and tried to back in. That didn't work either. "I'm terribly sorry, but either you have to grease me or Miss O'Day sits in the back."

For the first fifty or sixty miles, they couldn't get a conversation to last for more than a minute at a time unless it was about directions and route numbers. Finally, Si squirmed halfway around in his seat, trying to look at Sally with both eyes, but could only manage to turn far enough to see her with one.

"Miss O'Day, I have to ask you something. I tried asking Mashie over here, but that's like talking to a radish when something like this comes up. Okay?"

"On one condition, Mr. Sloan. From here on, you call me Sally and I call you Si. Unless you'd prefer Giant."

Si smiled. "Tell me, Sally, where do your parents think you are every night you go out with Mashie?"

"Jesus Christ," Murray said. He looked quickly at Si, then back out at the road ahead. "I mean, Jesus Christ."

"No, that's a fair question, Murray." Sally said. "They think I'm at political rallies, Si, sometimes at discussion groups, that sort of thing. Sinn Fein."

"You're kidding me," Murray said. "They don't know about me at all?"

"I don't believe this," Sally said. "And where does your family think you are?"

Suddenly, Murray had to change lanes, which took an extraordinary amount of concentration. He took a quick peek at Si, who was still torqued around in his seat and looked as though he might never be able to straighten out again.

"I mean it, Murray," Sally said. "Where?"

"All right, all right. I get the point."

"Where!"

"They think I'm with Si a lot, which we're looking for a place to open a market together. Or I'm playing poker a couple times a week. Work on the books."

"Boy," Sally said. "You too."

"Take a left here," Si said. The rest of the way, they talked about the Baer-Braddock fight, which was coming up in a couple months; they talked about the sorry Brooklyn Dodgers, who looked about as bad as last year except thank God for Van Lingle Mungo and Watty Clark; they listened to Sally talk about *Mutiny on the Bounty* and some discussion program she liked to listen to on the radio. They got a good twenty minutes of talk out of the Delaware River.

From the moment they entered the arena, nothing went right. The dressing room didn't have anything big enough for Si to lie down on except the floor, there wasn't enough tape, and the fight before Si's ended with a first round knockout so they had to hurry to get ready.

Murray knew Si was in trouble as soon as the opening bell rang. He wasn't moving right, as though he still had the weighted socks around his shoulders, and he was a half-second slow. The guy was nailing him with jabs. What was it, had they overtrained? Si was actually five pounds light because they thought he could use the extra sharpness, and maybe they'd done too much roadwork. Si missed a roundhouse right and almost flipped out of the ring.

Between the fourth and fifth rounds, Murray finally said, "What's wrong, Si? Just make him come to you and nail him with a left hook, he's wide open."

"There's nothing there, Mashie. Maybe I should sit on him."

Murray had never seen Si get knocked down before. Except for the Carnera fight, and all that knocked him down then was a promise. When Si hit the canvas on his back, arms flopping over his head, tears rushed into Murray's eyes, which astonished him even more than the sight of his friend prone and being counted out.

They ate dinner in a small café near the hotel—soup all around, since Si didn't feel like chewing and Murray and Sally weren't hungry. They sopped up the last bits with soft white bread, looking into their bowls, not speaking much.

Murray took care of room arrangements while Sally held Si by the elbow on the front stairs. Si stayed in a room down the hall from them. He bid them goodnight and walked slowly away, a hand up to wave, without really looking back.

Inside the room, Murray went directly over to the window and looked down at the street. Sally sat on the bed. He was still except for the clenching and unclenching of his hands.

"He'll be fine, Murray. Time alone's good for him tonight."

"Maybe. But did you see him there? I mean," he turned back to her, "Si on the floor, you know?"

"I know. Come here."

As he began to sit beside her, Sally turned toward Murray and wrapped her arms around him, pushing his back onto the bed while his legs dangled over the edge. She straddled him. She took off his glasses and leaned over his head to put them on the bedside table, her breasts moving across his face.

Murray reached up for her. Sally gripped his wrists, lowered his hands to the bed and spread them wide.

"Be still," she whispered.

"I . . ."

"Be still, Murray."

He woke up at about four and Sally was staring at him, her breast against his, her fingers tangled in his chest hair. They were still on top of the blanket, still naked.

"What?" he asked.

Sally closed her eyes. Gently, she shook her head and put it down against his shoulder.

"This was different," Murray said. "This was very different."

"Yes."

❦

One Sunday in early May of 1936, Murray drove Sally to the

south shore of Long Island for an afternoon at the beach. He'd been to this small resort town before and jogged along its boardwalk a few times with Si when they wanted someplace different for Sunday roadwork. Afterwards, they'd eat a couple dozen clams and drink beers on the bay side of town.

Today, though, was not about training or eating clams. In the evening, they would go to Murray's home and finally have dinner with his family. Emanuel and Sophia didn't seem surprised when Murray said he wanted to bring a girl home to meet them. Murray's sisters had long suspected he was seeing someone. It had been a topic of their dinnertime conversation for quite a while.

He took Sally's hand and led her east on the boardwalk. It was windy and cold for May. Sally's face was bright red before they'd walked two blocks.

"You wanna go into the Jackson there and have some coffee?" Murray asked. "Maybe this wasn't such a bright idea I had."

"I'm fine. Only let's get down onto the sand."

He led her down the ramp at the next corner and turned back to pass underneath the boardwalk. The sand there was dark gray and cold when they took off their shoes and socks. Once out from under the planks, though, the sand felt much warmer than the air. They headed east again, moving slowly through the softness.

"The water looks unbearable," Sally said.

"Not if you don't go into it."

"Murray, you have to use your imagination."

"I left it in the glove compartment. Look, Sally, I got a question for you."

She pulled him closer and put her arm around his waist. "And I have the answer: chopped liver. It's probably the only thing I refuse to eat and it's exactly what I think they're going to serve."

He stopped. "Which I been thinking about this for a long time, all right? I mean, would you wanna marry me?"

Murray could actually see the redness fade from her skin, as though he'd thrown bleach in her face instead of asked her to marry him. But wait, it wasn't that. What was happening was all the red from her face was seeping into her eyes.

"Mother of God, Murray."

"Hey, I don't speak Irish, remember? Does that mean yes or no?"

"Shouldn't we wait to see what your parents think? Or mine?"

"It won't matter."

Sally took a step to the side, still holding his hand. She looked away, watching a wave die out in foam. "Yes."

"You will?"

"No. I mean yes, I will. But I was saying yes, it will matter. To me, anyway."

For the rest of the afternoon, they were shy together. It wasn't how Murray thought it would be, after you asked a girl to marry you. They drove back into Brooklyn early, got dressed early, and arrived at the Perlman's apartment forty minutes ahead of schedule. From the hallway they could smell the roasting chickens. No liver, he was sure of it.

As though they knew he'd be early, Emanuel and Sophia were fully dressed and standing together in the foyer when Murray opened the door and led Sally in. Emanuel had on his best cardigan, a deep piney green one, and Sophia wore the ruffly blue dress with millions of buttons that Murray always loved. He was deeply touched.

After the introductions, they went into the living room where Murray's sisters were waiting for them—Hannah, Charlotte, and even Bella, who was married and lived in Trenton. Of course, his brothers Herb and Joseph were not there. That would have been too much. A wedding, they show up, or a funeral, but this was just to meet a girl they didn't know he'd been seeing for over two years. Of course, Murray hadn't brought home many girls at all.

"So tell me, dear," Sophia said when they had all been introduced and served their crackers. "Where did you two meet?"

"In New Jersey, Mrs. Perlman. I was at a function there with my brother."

Oh, very good, Murray thought. There's plenty of time to talk boxing.

The evening went splendidly. Bella knew about the issues of Irish unification and British colonialism. Charlotte had read *Gone with the Wind*. Hannah was the same size as Sally and also loved to sew. Murray stole glances at his parents, who were smiling as though he'd brought home someone named Rose Goldberg.

Emanuel was waiting for him when Murray returned after driving Sally home. It was 2:00 a.m.

"Pop, you waited up."

Emanuel nodded. "Your mother and I wanted you to know how pleased we are that you brought Miss O'Day home to meet us. And she's a lovely young lady, I can see why you're attracted to her."

"It's more than that, you know. We've been seeing a lot of each other."

"I thought as much."

Murray walked past his father into the dining room and sat

198

at his usual dinnertime place. "It's. I'm. We're pretty serious." He looked down the table as though wondering where the succotash had gone. "I want to marry her, Pop."

"You do." Emanuel sat at the table's head and folded his hands where his plate should be. "I can certainly understand why, too, seeing her and listening to her. Very sharp, she is. But you know it would be impossible."

Murray looked at him. "It's 1936, Pop. Brooklyn, not Krakow."

"This I know. But in our family, Murray, you cannot do what you're thinking of doing." He spread his hands on the table. "Cannot do it."

"I'm twenty-eight years old. I own a business."

"In a building that I own, Murray."

Emanuel was watching the kitchen door as though expecting Sophia to emerge with a platter of flanken. Murray was looking across the table, to where his sister Charlotte used to sit and gorge herself with food while talking about losing weight.

"What are you saying, Pop?"

"Only what you heard, Murray. Nothing more or less."

"If I don't listen to you I'm outta business? That's what you're saying, right?"

Emanuel's brows jerked, but otherwise he was still. "You know, your mother and I, we feel there should be no confusion over how our grandchildren will be brought up when we're gone. We feel that it's best for everyone that we stay together, the family. That's what I'm saying."

e⌢

199

What a spring, what a summer. Travel was on everyone's minds, getting away, moving on, going fast as possible. Down in Lakehurst, New Jersey, not an hour away from Murray's market, the zeppelin *Hindenburg* burst into flames at its tower mooring. People in midtown Manhattan who wanted to see where thirty-five zeppelin passengers and crew had died could take the new Lincoln Tunnel under the Hudson River and surface in Weehawken five minutes later. When Murray first drove through the tunnel to look at a new supplier of fowl, he held his breath almost the whole way. Meanwhile, out on the west coast, the Golden Gate Bridge opened and somewhere in the South Pacific Amelia Earhart disappeared in her little plane. Howard Hughes was flying around the world in less than four days. But Murray knew there was no place to go.

When he told Sally they couldn't see each other again, it was as though she already knew what he was going to say. She kissed him passionately and ran her fingers along his cheek about where her own scar would be if it were on his face.

"It matters," she said. "I always knew it matters."

FRESH MINT

The shoes Fitz wears are a model closed out by Nike five years ago. But they still look brand new on him because he hardly moves.

His racquetball game is all waves, all junk shots and marginalia. He plays the ceiling and dead spots. He detects irregularities in your breathing from across the court and always knows where you are. Granted, the guy's obese. But go ahead, try to get one by him.

e⁓

He can't be five-five, and he looks like a goal-line stand. I resemble a sprig of mint that reaches all the way to the bottom of your julep glass or, in certain lights and shirts, a swizzle stick.

To look at us, you'd think Fitz is the Senator and I'm the lobbyist. But we're cast against type, at least physically. If I had to do what he does, I'd starve.

It used to be that a lobbyist lobbied in a lobby. Or you'd go outside the chambers and there he'd be, elbow on the shiny brass rail, looking down at the tourists lining the rotunda. Nowadays it's a game of papers and printouts, numbers more than words.

Racquetball instead of duck hunting.

Thank God for Fitz. There's a lot of subjects he would never bring up because there's no need to: I know who contributed what to my campaign, I know the various interests Fitz agrees to represent. So he still talks Seattle Mariners, he talks snow pack on Mount Bachelor, talks salmon runs.

Fitz has been at this for years. In committee rooms, in the chambers, at the rear table in the cafeteria. The perfect lobbyist. They say bamboo under the fingernails wouldn't get Fitz to reveal Word One about his deals. January through June, I see him more than I see my family.

We've always gotten along.

This time, though, I knew there was something special on his mind. He didn't even want to talk about the Portland high school quarterback who just signed with UCLA instead of going to Oregon. Instead, Fitz said *Let's play a set of racquetball.*

The racquetball club is his real office. It's where he lines things up, where he closes deals. On the court is where he drills you into going easy on him.

How about this?, he'll offer. A little lob shot.

No? Well, maybe you'll go for one of these. Front wall–side wall–back wall.

Smash a shot off his naked back, he says "my serve" and never winces. Run around him and miss a return because of it, he says "was I in your way?" and offers up the ball.

Nah, I say. You're up.

e⌒

So I get the first five points. I sprint the court, bounce off the side walls, climb the back wall like this is jai alai. Fitz is crimson.

"Five zip," I tell him.

"So who's the Muslim?" he gasps. "Your mother or your father?"

I hold the ball and look at him. "What're you talking about, Muslim?"

"The way you play, there's got to be some dervish in you. Has to come from someplace, right? They're Muslim. Jeez, I bet you're a hell of a dancer."

"Five zip."

"You already said that, Senator Woodley."

e⌒

Fitz wants my vote. I mean, we're not in here for our hearts.

In the locker room, I found out he's working on the speed-limit bill for my old enemy, Senator Hale Buddin. All they need is one crossover from our side to carry the Buddin Bill. Right now, the vote's fifteen-fifteen. With me, it'd be sixteen-fourteen.

Usually, I stick with my party caucus. But I never liked driving fifty-five and I don't wear a seat belt and I don't like the idea that we can pass a law to make me—or anybody—do these things.

So I told Fitz that I'd listen. Even if it means I might have to vote with Hale Buddin.

Fitz always works for an odd mix. This time, he hooked up with a group of truckers and oil companies and traveling salesmen, and they got the Minority Leader to carry the bill. That's where

Fitz comes in. He goes back a long way with Mr. Minority Leader Hale Buddin. I'm sure the only thing they ever played together was poker.

While we were tying our shoes, I allowed as how I could use some help with a bill of my own. Senate Bill 3312. It would declare peppermint the State Herb and it's been stuck in Hale Buddin's committee for three months.

This is vital stuff. Being State Herb would exempt peppermint from the shipping tax. See, I farm a little mint when I'm not busy being a Senator.

e

Fitz breaks my service with a drop-dead fluke that catches the crease between front wall and ceiling. I'm against the back wall, but up on my toes. Just miss it with my dive.

He offers a hand to help me up, then walks over to fetch the ball. He rests a foot on it, backspins it onto his toes, kicks it in the air, and catches it.

"Anyone can do that," I say.

He smiles and flips me the ball. "Oh-nine?"

"Oh-ten. Nice try, though."

His first serve hits high off the wall, lands in front of me where I'm riveted to the court waiting for his slammer, and bloops over my head. He never even looks.

"One-ten." He sounds sorry.

e

I get it. He plans on volleying me to death. Nothing I do fools him. A little spin here, the ceiling there, a deep lob. And he gets everything without moving.

"Six-ten," he says.

It seems like an hour's passed.

I haven't gotten to serve again. Fitz sighs, bounces the ball, looks back at me, looks forward, crouches.

This shot is never higher than six inches above the floor. It's by me before I can react.

"Seven-ten."

$e \frown$

I beat him, but not really. It was nineteen-eighteen mine for a dozen changes of service. Then all of a sudden he couldn't reach two deep shots, the kind he'd had no trouble reaching before.

Give me some credit, Fitz.

We duck out of the court to get water between games. The corridor is empty.

"You say mint?" he holds the water on, motions for me to drink first.

"Mint."

"Now here's a real coincidence. Senator Buddin likes mint. I mean, the man likes all kinds of mint. Peppermint, spearmint, doublemint, the works."

"You know, we're the country's leading producer of mint," I tell him.

"You mean we, Oregon, or we, the Woodleys?"

"Well, I do some business."

"So does the Senator."

He holds the door open for me so I can get back into the court. The ball is smack in the middle, like it's been placed there by an official.

"Loser serves," I say.

❧

Game Two he opens with ten points in a row, mostly off of my mistakes. I give him three backhands right at his side, belt high, which he puts away with no trouble. A shot off the rim of my racket that never makes the wall. That kind of thing.

I break his service but then double-fault. I misjudge a shot that hits me in the shoulder.

"You aren't just being nice, are you?" he asks.

❧

I change my grip. This works.

Speed and power will beat desperate finesse time and time again. If it's in control.

Now I understand. I've been out of control.

I start getting to his shots, no matter where they are. I keep Fitz in front of me. I move the ball on him.

We're at twenty-twenty and it's his serve. He turns his whole body to face me. I shrug myself off the back wall so he won't see me resting.

"All even," he says.

I nod. "New game."

"Gotta win by two."

"I know how to keep score."

He turns. He bounces the ball a few times.

❧

"Rubber game?" he asks.

"It'll have to be quick. Those two took us almost the whole hour."

"No problem. The hard part's over." He smiles at me. "We know each other's game now."

❧

Arms down, mouth gaping, Fitz lets the shower run directly on his bald head. His face remains seven shades redder than the rest of him. Soap pools at his hips, swirls off his thighs.

"So what do you think?" he asks.

I don't know if he means about the games we played or about the votes. I'm sure he intends it that way.

"We'll have to do this again," I say.

"Not this year, we won't. That is, unless you develop a sudden interest in tort reform, which sounds like a dessert to me. From now on, I live and breathe tort reform. Session's over in two weeks. This is my last day to worry about speed limits."

"Jesus, that's right, Only two more weeks left. Back in the winter, it didn't look like we'd have so much to do. Some big bills are still around."

"Don't I know it, too." He looks up, takes a mouthful of water and gargles. "Big bills, they're my living, Senator."

I can't see him. My eyes are shut now while I rinse out the shampoo.

"So there's not a lot of time left," he says, getting back to his point.

"Enough."

"That's true." He seems to gather his energies as if for one last serve. "And then comes the summer and I get to watch Cubs games again."

I ask, "What does the Senator like to drink in the summertime?"

"Same as in wintertime. His mar-toonys."

"Is that right? Gin or vodka?"

"Vodka." He turns away from me, twists the faucet for more cold water. I open my eyes and see him shake all over like a sea lion. "But he'll drink gin in a pinch."

"He ever try a sprig of mint in his martini?"

Fitz smiles. I can feel it, though I can't see it.

"Mint? I don't believe so. Always has his toonys with a twist."

"Doesn't know what he's missing."

"Maybe that's because he never gets fresh mint." Fitz shuts off the water and staggers out of the shower toward his towel. "Now if you were to drive down and see him next month, you could bring him some fresh, couldn't you? Would be very fresh, I'd think, if you were doing sixty-five."

"That would work," I say and shut off my shower.

REPLACEMENT PLAYERS

I thought, *why not?* I wasn't doing anything else at the time. It was only a four-hour drive up to Seattle, where the Mariners were holding their tryout camp at the Kingdome, and we'd just put new tires on the car.

Didn't look like the players and owners would settle the strike in time for spring training, so teams were holding tryout camps. I'd never make the cut, and the pros weren't picketing, so it would be a lark. Sure, I was in my forties, but teams were talking about bringing back older players. I'd seen pictures in the paper of guys who looked as though they'd gained more weight since retiring than I weighed altogether, guys who had a lot more gray hair than I do under the 1911 New York Yankees cap my wife Meredith got me for Valentine's Day. Hell, I've had gray hair since I was twenty-nine, especially in my beard.

For the past six years, I'd been disabled by a rare neurological disorder, one of those diseases that's named after the physician who discovered it but died before he could figure out a cure. As long as I didn't get too fatigued, and didn't try to do too much at any one time or for too long, and provided that I followed a few simple management procedures, most of the worst symptoms could be held in check. Sometimes my world listed a bit to the left, but I'd learned how to compensate for that. In the batter's box, hitting curve balls could be tricky, because they'd probably make me dizzy, but lots of guys can't hit curve balls. Playing second base, I might have trouble going back under a pop fly, especially if I put my arms out to the side while looking up at the ball the way I was trained to do, because then I'd simply fall down. Same thing if I held my feet together and closed my eyes, but once I got past the national anthem I couldn't imagine a time I'd do that during the game. There could also be some difficulty with the coach's signals, since my short-term memory is erratic these days, or with concentrating if the fans made too much noise. But I figured I could face those problems when I got to them. Besides, there probably wouldn't be many fans anyway.

Look, I'll be honest, I could use the money. What I was getting from Social Security and from my former employer made it so we ate a lot of tuna-helper after about the twenty-third of the month. Plus, I used to play some ball, back before I got sick. Actually, back before I graduated from college, but the big league scouts were always around and I thought I had a shot until that one game where I struck out five times. Still. Meredith and I always went up to watch the Mariners play several times a season and I have to tell you I could play as well as some of those jokers. Meredith said so too and she hadn't even seen me play. But she'd seen me at the batting ranges, where I could still spray line drives from both sides of the plate. I never lost the touch, even in the cages with the eighty m.p.h. machines. The way I figured it, there wouldn't be too many guys throwing faster than that among the replacement players.

But it wasn't just the money, of course. Playing big-league ball was something I always dreamed of doing, ever since I was a kid in Brooklyn, New York, going to Ebbets Field to watch the Dodgers. I have very clear memories of being there in 1957, sitting just to the first base side of home plate, watching the Dodgers finish out their Brooklyn lives. Across the left field wall there were all those signs—The Brass Rail, Schaefer Beer, Luckies, Buy Tydol—and then Gino Cimoli or Sandy Amoros beside the 351 ft. sign against left-handed batters. Yeah, I'd be happy with just one game, one time at bat, one grounder cleanly fielded.

When we pulled into the Kingdome parking lot that morning, I thought, *well I guess I'm not the only one.* Meredith just laughed once, that wonderful guffaw of hers, then got hold of herself and wove her way through the crowded lot to the handicapped parking area right next to the entrance. She seemed as happy as I was.

"Maybe you'd better leave your cane in the car," she said.

This was something I'd already thought of myself. I mean, give me some credit. I zipped open my bag and checked everything one more time: mitt, shoes, batting gloves, lucky tee-shirt, the small crystal that Meredith gave me for luck. I took a couple of my noon-hour pills a little early, so no one would have to see me doing it inside, and we were ready to go. She leaned over to give me a kiss, then tugged down her Mariners cap, slipped on her Joe Carter mitt so she could catch foul balls, threw her sweater over her shoulders, and we got out. At the gate, she took out her camera and got a good shot of me heading down the ramp toward the clubhouse.

"Break a leg, Shooter," she shouted after me. Meredith used

to be an actress and she doesn't know much about baseball, but that didn't stop her from giving me her full support. Or using the wrong nickname. On the ride up to Seattle, I'd confessed that in school my teammates called me Scooter.

Getting to the clubhouse was like passing through customs at the airport in Damascus. Once they were sure I didn't have any contraband in my bag, and once I'd spent a half-hour filling out all their forms—no, I wouldn't sue the Mariners if I died as a result of the tryout—and trying not to exaggerate my baseball accomplishments, I was given number 49 to pin on my shirt and was waved through to the inner sanctum. I don't think anyone saw me bump into the door jamb as I walked in.

The only thing that surprised me about the locker room was how small it seemed. I thought modern players had all these contractual agreements giving them a quarter-mile of airspace between each other or something. Hot tubs and massage tables and a spate of Nautilus machines. I thought there would be director's chairs or padded recliners by every locker.

I also thought there would be a more even distribution among the guys who were trying out. But most of them, a good eighty percent or more, were half my age, a few of them polite enough not to stare and then turn back to their lockers gagging down their laughter. But only a few. There seemed to be a grandfather's corner over by the coach's office, where I saw three guys who probably could remember Timothy Leary or knew Frankie Lymon and the Teenagers weren't a neighborhood gang. They were carefully pulling on their stirrup socks and lacing their shoes, none of which were as clean as mine.

"Hey, how you doing?" I said, trying to sound crusty. Also

trying to keep my vocabulary simple enough so I wouldn't end up saying the wrong word. Earlier in the day, I'd generously informed Meredith that we were in the *excerpts* of Seattle instead of the *outskirts.*

One of the younger older guys knocked his bag off a stool and shoved the rickety three-legger over toward me. Another guy opened a locker next to the one he was using and took out his equipment so I could use that locker. The third member of the group looked familiar enough that I wondered if he was a retired player, somebody whose face I'd seen in *The Sporting News* a few years back.

"No," he said, before I asked. "I just look like the fella. Odell Jones. He played for six different teams in nine years and had the absolute worst season of his illustrious career right here in Seattle. The General Manager called me *Odell* when he came by a few minutes ago and said he was glad to see me back. I just shook his hand and nodded—far be it from me to correct the man. Maybe I'll make the team if I keep my mouth shut around the coaching staff. Later they'll be too embarrassed to drop me."

"What did I miss so far?" I asked.

"Nothing," the guy who was not Odell Jones said. "No one said a thing to us all morning. Except the little old clubhouse guy keeps telling us not to throw anything on the floor and if we have the runs we should clean the throne ourselves. That notice over by the water cooler says tryouts begin at 11:00."

I guessed I should be able to get my shoes tied in the next half hour, especially if I didn't try to talk at the same time, so I nodded and turned toward my locker. A few of the younger men were filing out and heading toward a passage that must have led onto the field. Within five minutes, the place was deserted except for the three of us geezers.

The one sitting next to me started talking as though we'd been having a conversation all morning. "So I told her you can come or you can stay, makes no difference to me, but I'm going to Seattle. You know what she does?" He looked at me, his socks dangling from both hands as though he wasn't sure whether to put them on or use them to strangle me.

I shook my head and started searching diligently for my cap.

"Only closes down the bank account, packs up and drives to her mother in Sacramento, that's all. I had to take the damn train up here and borrow a hundred bucks from my brother. How am I supposed to play major league-quality ball when she does this to me? I don't make the team now, I know whose fault it is."

"Shoot," not-Odell Jones said. "My old lady doesn't know where I'm at. Probably thinks I took off for some meeting and forgot to leave her a note. She's cool."

"What do you do?" I asked, mostly as an excuse to turn away from my neighbor, who was still staring at me, maybe wondering if I had given his wife the idea about Sacramento.

"Software. I write those manuals tell you how to use a program. And play in the softball leagues around town. I hit ninety homers last summer."

"Was relaxed, I could hit me a few taters," my neighbor mumbled. "I could probably hit one clear out of this place. Say, any you guys got something help a person relax?"

Finally the oldest of us, the one who hadn't said anything yet, slammed his locker shut and turned to the rest of us. He had on an old Seattle Pilots hat and a purple University of Washington sweat suit, and his face was all grim lines and odd shadows, like a charcoal sketch of a cubist portrait. His high voice was a shock coming out of such a long, cowboy body.

"You know what this is?" He waited, a professor giving us adult-ed students plenty of time to frame our answers, then sadly nodded as though he knew all along how dumb we really were. "Only the most important day of my life, that's all. I am not here to dink around, get cut and go back to Yakima so I can tell my drinking buddies about my grand adventure. This is no adolescent fantasy for me, so I don't want to hear any more talk about your fastballs and your home runs. I've had enough." He stalked out of the locker room, pounding a ball into his mitt, and we could still hear him talking as he disappeared from view.

Not-Odell Jones looked at my neighbor, who was tying his shoes, and then at me. He shrugged. "I hope they got a doctor on call."

I waited till the other two oldsters had left, saying I needed a couple minutes in private, and went over to the full length mirror by the showers. Hate to say this, but I really looked all right, if a little tired around the eyes. You'd never know I was brain-damaged, especially if I wasn't trying to copy your movements or follow complicated directions. Last month, to get me in shape for this, Meredith bought an exercise video and we popped it into the VCR. Here were these supple young kids hopping around behind a woman who looked a lot like not-Odell Jones, and she was hollering out directions, saying *now turn left* while turning to my right, saying *right arm to left ankle* like we're playing "Simon Says" but then dropping the arm that was on my left, till I just had to sit down on the couch and watch Meredith rock 'n' roll.

Anyway, I looked all right, so I picked up a bat that was leaning against the first locker by the door. I took my usual lefty batting stance and glared at an imaginary pitcher, then shifted my weight and took a smooth inside-out cut, the bat ending up in my right hand pointing toward the bathroom, a perfect swing. I was ready.

At the mouth of the stairway leading into the dugout, I practiced what my occupational therapist had taught me long ago. I stopped to get my bearings, noticing the layout before me, the obstacles in my path, and studied the steps up onto the field. *Four short steps,* I told myself. That way I would have a better chance of not falling on my face.

When I trotted out to the field, I could clearly hear Meredith screaming for me from behind the dugout. I knew she was snapping pictures too. If I wasn't being so cool, I would have trotted over and given her a kiss of thanks for steady support.

As soon as I crossed into the outfield, not-Odell Jones tossed a ball to me. I caught it and threw it back before realizing that I was thinking about something else, about how hard the astroturf felt and how strangely sound moved down there on the playing field. Damn, I was lucky the ball didn't hit me in the face.

"Feeling all right?" I yelled to him. But he wouldn't answer. I'd forgotten that he didn't want to speak in front of the coaches. "Sorry."

They broke us into two groups of about forty each, half moving toward the left field foul line and half toward right. Time for the sprints. We had to run past these old guys with stopwatches, scouts or personnel staff or auditors, I don't know who they were.

I hadn't thought about having to race. Let me hit, fellas. Let me field some grounders. I used to be fast. I used to have all my hair, too, but those were qualities that I was losing before I got sick. Hey, forty yards isn't that far, right?

When the whistle blew, I got a good start and simply refused to let myself look anywhere but at the ground right in front of me. Good thing Meredith and I had jogged together to the mailbox and back all month, an easy quarter-mile, because my leg muscles were in fairly decent shape now and I didn't pull anything. Amazing: I got past the scouts in just under six seconds. Anybody who came in over six seconds had to run it again and after three tries was dismissed from the tryout. I immediately went to the center field wall and sat with my back against it, watching the action. Not-Odell Jones made it on his second try, as did the guy from Yakima. I saw my neighbor walking toward the dugout with his mitt on his head like a cap and was doubly thrilled not to be going to the locker room.

After the speed test, there were about fifty of us left. We had to throw to each other, one group standing at the outfield wall, the other standing just beyond the infield dirt. Twenty minutes later there were about forty left.

I was getting very tired and hoped they'd let me hit while I could still stand. They split us into three groups this time, sending ten toward home plate for their turns at bat. The rest were split into pitchers, who went to the bullpen with a coach, and fielders who had to catch whatever came their way. Fortunately, I was among the ten batters. The fielders had to concentrate not only on what we hit, but also on balls being hit to them by coaches. I didn't want to think about having to go out there after finishing my swings.

Suddenly I heard Meredith cheering for me again. She'd

moved from behind the dugout to behind home plate. I hadn't heard a thing for the last half hour.

The guy from Yakima took his place in the batter's box. He looked good up there, the bat waggling high above his head, his knees slightly flexed. I was impressed, but the batting practice pitcher wasn't—the first pitch was very close to his head and sent him reeling backwards out of the box.

I could just imagine him saying, "I've had enough." He dug in exactly where he'd been standing before and started waggling the bat again. The next pitch, a low fastball, he golfed into deep left field, a major league shot. He hit the next one directly back at the pitcher, who was protected by a screen but nevertheless ducked automatically, which set loose a round of friendly jeering from the coaches. Yakima was impressive. He drilled the next three pitches, one each to left, center and right. On his last swing, he gave it everything he had, the angriest and most ferocious cut I ever hope to see. The ball went straight up and seemed to get lost in the gray paint of the dome before reappearing as it came down behind third base. He stormed out of the box toward the outfield, cursing himself for overswinging, and made a wide loop around the coaches. I never saw him again.

When it was my turn to hit, I found myself both relaxed and fully focused. Better get through it before things start swirling on me. The pitcher was left-handed, so I went over to hit right-handed, which was always my better side anyway. Things were falling into place. The first pitch went by so fast I didn't have time to notice anything except the hiss the ball made in the instant before it popped into the catcher's mitt. I stepped out to regain my composure, squeezed the bat between my hands, adjusted my batting gloves, and stepped back in. The next pitch was a hard curve, which I could see fairly well but didn't even think about swinging at. As the ball broke downwards and out of the strike zone, I followed the flight with my eyes, almost staggering across the plate after it. If this was *The Gong Show*, I thought, I was about to get gonged. What was with this pitcher? Was he still mad at my friend from Yakima and taking it out on me?

His next pitch was a fastball, but slightly slower than the first one and I swung at it, fouling the pitch straight back. It looped directly toward the area where Meredith had been standing. I spun around to watch it, losing my balance and teetering toward third base, but could just see her reach up with her gloved hand and catch the ball before I hit the ground. Oh man, we got a souvenir, bless her sweet soul.

"Nice swing, 49," someone yelled from behind me. "Now straighten it out."

I dusted myself off and got ready to step back in. Suddenly I realized that, whatever else happened today, it didn't really matter. I was exhausted and dizzy, but I'd done it. With Meredith's help, I'd come up to Seattle when it didn't seem like I'd ever be able to travel again. I'd made it most of the way through the tryouts, gotten to hit, and made contact with a good fastball. We had pictures and a ball to take home with us, but of course that wasn't really the point. The point was what was now inside my head, along with the bizarre image now forming of the pitching mound as it drifted toward third base. Indeed, the entire field was beginning to rearrange itself in my vision, as fields do when I am tired, and I knew it was time to call it quits.

I looked out toward the center field stands, where Meredith

and I preferred sitting so we could catch home runs during Mariners games, though we'd never actually managed to snag one. Then I took a deep breath and, using the bat as a cane, walked over to the stands behind home plate. By the time I got there, Meredith had come down toward the field and was waiting for me, arms wide, tears in her eyes, her face open in an enormous smile.

I waved the next batter into the box, then made my way slowly into the locker room to shower and change. As I was drying myself, not-Odell Jones came in and slumped on the stool in front of his locker.

"Cat's out of the bag," he said. "Even with my mouth shut, they figured out I wasn't Odell Jones as soon as they saw I threw lefty."

"That's too bad."

"I told them I hit ninety homers last summer. But it was too late, man."

"Did you get to bat?"

"Yeah, but I left my stroke home. Hit nothing but air."

I took his phone number and promised to call sometime. His real name was Reese Morgan and he lived less than an hour from us. I thought Meredith would like him. She was waiting for me at the main gate, popping the ball into her glove and singing her favorite song, "Try a Little Tenderness." She didn't hear me coming because of the echo her voice made in the concrete hallway. I snatched the ball out of the air, backed up a step, bent at the knees and joined her in song: "You got to, you got to, you got to…"

ACKNOWLEDGMENTS

The stories in this book, sometimes in different forms, originally appeared in the following magazines:

Aethlon: The Journal of Sport Literature, "The Cage"

Crab Orchard Review, "Karaoke Night at the Trail's End" (as "Crazy") and "Let Us Rejoice!"

Glimmer Train Stories, "The Fights" and "The Royal Family"

North American Review, "The Peanut Vendor," "Shorefront Manor," and "The Tour"

Ontario Review, "Plans"

Tampa Review, "Devoted to You"

Tikkun, "Cream of Kohlrabi"

Virginia Quarterly Review, "Replacement Players" and "The Wings of the Wind"

Witness: Aging in America Issue, "The Wanderer"

Witness: Sports in America Issue, "Fresh Mint"

"Alzheimer's Noir" originally appeared in the anthology *Portland Noir* (Akashic Books, 2009).

"The Cage" was included in *Bottom of the Ninth: Great Contemporary Baseball Short Stories* (Southern Illinois University Press, 2003).

"The Royal Family" was included in *Signatures: An Anthology for Writers* (Mayfield Publishing Company, 1998).

"The Wings of the Wind" was included in *Touched By Adoption* (Green River Press, 1999), *Blue Cathedral: Short Fiction for the New Millennium* (Red Hen Press, 2000), and also *Writing the Future: Progress and Evolution* (The MIT Press, 2004).

I am grateful to Oregon Literary Arts and the Oregon Arts Commission for fellowships during the time when these stories were written.